# THE CASE OF THE
# INTENTIONAL
## ACCIDENT

## a mac & sam mystery

A NOVEL BY

# DEBORAH SPRINKLE

*To all the men and women of the police forces around the world who risk their lives in order to keep us safe.*

# CHAPTER 1

The soul-piercing scream shattered her concentration a second before the lights went out. Private Investigator Mackenzie Love groped for her cellphone, pressed Flashlight, and did a sweep of the historic museum's research room, her heart pounding in her chest. Metal shelves filled with books of varying sizes slid in and out of view, but no monsters—human or otherwise—appeared in the narrow ray of light.

Excited voices reached her from the hall outside. She grabbed her bag and went in search of the commotion. As she turned the corner, a flashlight beam hit her square in the face. "Ouch." She threw her arm up to shade her eyes.

"Oh dear, Mackenzie." Mrs. White lowered the offending light. "Something terrible has happened."

"I figured as much." Mac blinked and rubbed her eyes. "What's going on?"

"Mr. James has been electrocuted."

Mac stared at the historian. "But Doug's been an electrician for twenty years."

"I know." The older woman took hold of her arm. "Come

see for yourself. One of our volunteers is a nurse. She's with him now."

A group of men and women stood outside the door to the copy room. At the back, a man in khakis and a blue shirt stood on tiptoe, craning his neck to see over the heads of the crowd.

"I told them not to go in." Mrs. White cleared a path using a firm tone of voice and a touch on a shoulder. "Excuse us, please." She patted Mac on the arm. "While you're in there, I'll see if I can get the lights back on. I feel much better with you here."

An acrid smell made Mac wrinkle her brow. She inspected the space with her flashlight. The room was oblong, with the short ends to the right and left. Two copy machines, a worktable, a bookcase, and a wall of file cabinets filled the space. A metal ladder stood to one side. Wires hung from the ceiling.

Douglas James lay on his back in the glow of a small lantern. A woman performed CPR, and her soft counting rose above the low hum of voices behind Mac.

"Twenty-eight, twenty-nine, thirty." She sat back on her heels and shook out her arms. Her pale blue eyes glinted with unshed tears.

"Want me to take over?"

She started. "Yes. Hurry. I'm tired."

Mac dropped to Doug's side and began the compressions. *Two hands, fingers interlocked, center of the chest, just below the breastbone, press at least two inches down, thirty compressions.* She'd forgotten how hard it was.

She lost count when the lights popped on and paused to examine Doug.

"Show me a glimpse of those warm brown eyes," the nurse muttered under her breath.

But his eyelids didn't flutter, and the skin of his clean-shaven face and almost bald head seemed to grow paler by the minute.

"We'll alternate until the paramedics get here," the woman said, her voice choked with emotion as she started pressing on his chest.

Mac nodded, but she could tell Doug was already gone. She glanced at the woman, so focused on her task. When was it okay to let go? To leave things as they were?

She'd come to the history museum to research the years right before her parents' deaths because she was determined to find out how they died. But did she truly want to know? Was it worth the effort? Or, now that she was engaged, should she learn to live in the present and look to the future? A woman's cry of anguish brought her to her feet.

"I want to see him. He's my husband."

Laura James. Mac crossed to the door in time to block the stricken woman as she broke through the crowd outside.

"I tried to keep her out." Mrs. White lifted her arms in a useless gesture. "My dear, let them help Douglas." She tried in vain to urge the younger woman toward the door.

Mac held her in a tight grip, but the woman was strong. She wasn't sure how much longer she could hold her back. "You need to let us take care of him until the ambulance—"

Two EMTs pushed through into the room.

Laura stopped struggling and Mac guided her to a chair in the hall, where the woman buried her face in her hands.

"I'm so sorry." Mac sat next to her. What should she do? She hated to leave the upset woman alone, but she barely knew her. She searched the small crowd for anyone who looked as if they might be a friend, but saw no one.

Laura sat hunched over, her hair covering her face, for a while. With a sigh, she straightened and brushed her long black hair over her shoulder. "Do you have a tissue?"

"Yes." Mac dug in her bag and handed it to her. The woman wasn't wearing a wedding ring. Maybe she dressed in a hurry this morning? Mac eyed Laura's designer shoes, stylish outfit, and expensive necklace and earrings. Then again ...

She followed Mac's look. "It's being cleaned." She handed the tissue back.

"Sorry. I didn't mean to be that obvious." Mac felt the heat rise on her neck. "I just got engaged. But we haven't gotten our rings yet." The crumpled tissue was dry. She tossed it into the trash and continued to study the grieving woman.

For a fortyish woman, she was strikingly beautiful, with the high cheekbones of a model, smooth, tan skin, and large black eyes framed by long lashes. But no trail of tears marred her perfect face.

Mac's departed mother whispered in her mind's ear. *"Don't be too quick to judge. Not everyone cries when they're grieving."*

"Good luck." Laura's tone was not one of joy. "I mean, congratulations on your engagement."

A man rushed over, his face filled with compassion. "Laura, what's happened?"

"Douglas is dead." Laura rose to greet him. "He's been electrocuted."

The hairs stood up on the back of Mac's neck. How could Laura know her husband was dead? Had she said anything to give the woman that idea? Mac reviewed the brief words they'd shared. No, she hadn't. Then what made the woman so sure?

Mac got to her feet. The man wore khaki pants and a blue shirt. She'd seen him before—in the hallway outside the copy room just after Doug's accident. A full head of silver hair over a youthful face made it hard to determine his age.

"Are you sure?" He grasped Laura's arms.

"No, but he looked so gray." Laura crossed her arms in front of her. "And he wasn't moving." She turned to Mac. "You were there. What do you think?"

What should she say? Her mama always said it was best to answer with honesty. She was ninety-nine percent sure Doug was dead, but ...

"Jake." Laura's eyes brightened, and she rushed down the hall. "Thank you for coming. Did you hear it on your scanner?"

Detective Jake Sanders caught the woman before she could throw her arms around him. "The police are always called out when there's an accident of this nature. I'm sorry about Doug."

Mac raised her eyebrows at him. Was this yet another woman besotted with her fiancé? First Zoe and now Laura. Jake came over to Mac and pulled her in for a hug.

"How are you?" He kissed her on the lips, something he never did in public when on duty.

"Oh." Laura looked from Mac to Jake. "You didn't say you were engaged to Jake."

"Yes." She patted his chest and fluttered her eyelashes at him. Barf.

"Well." Laura backed away. "Congratulations again."

"Make way." The emergency medical personnel pushed through the door to the copy room with Doug strapped to a gurney. An oxygen mask covered his face, and an IV bag lay on his chest. The nurse doing CPR followed close behind.

"Doug." Laura rushed after them.

"I need to go." The man in the blue shirt turned to Mac.

For a moment, his public mask slipped, and Mac realized he was older than she'd thought. Maybe in his early forties? And one other thing. He loved Laura James.

He offered her his card. "I'm Thomas Underwood, Doug's partner. Thanks for all your help."

Where had Mac heard that name before?

# CHAPTER 2

Jake had never had trouble getting dates, but since his engagement, it seemed like he'd become ... what did they call it? A chick magnet? He hated it. All he wanted was to do his job and spend his free time with Mackenzie. Was that too much to ask?

"Laura comes to the gun range." He stepped in front of Mac and looked her full in the face.

"What?" She furrowed her brow at him.

"Laura." He took her hand. "That's how she knows me."

"I've given up on that." She waved a hand in the air. "You're just a chick magnet."

That phrase again. "No. I'm. not." He dropped her hand.

"Okayyy." She held up her hands in surrender. "Sorry."

"I'm your fiancé. That's it." He straightened his shirt. "Walk me through what happened." He followed Mac to the copy room, where she described the scene, indicated where Doug lay on the floor, and detailed administering CPR.

"What's the nurse's name?"

"I don't know. We'll have to ask Mrs. White."

Jake took notes. For a history museum, there was a lot of present-day drama happening here. A few months ago, a man was shot on the bench against the wall. Now, another man badly hurt updating the wiring. He shook his head. Poor Mrs. White. "We need to find her."

"She's probably in her office." Mac led the way.

Mrs. White motioned them in and indicated two chairs in front of her desk. "I'm so glad to see you, Detective Sanders. This has me so flustered."

"I understand." Jake gave her a sympathetic smile. "There are just a few things I need from you." He looked at his notes. "First, who found the—Doug?" He'd almost said 'body.'

"One of the ladies who volunteers here regularly. Francis Underwood."

Jake cut his eyes to Mac. Underwood. "Is she married to Thomas Underwood?"

"No, no. She's his sister." Mrs. White looked at Mac. "She's the nurse who did CPR on poor Douglas, dear."

Mac nodded, her teeth worrying her bottom lip.

Something was bothering her. Jake made a note to find out what. He focused once more on his questions. "Who turned the lights on?"

"Our maintenance man. He went back to where the breaker box is and flipped a switch." Mrs. White lifted folded hands in the air. "Praise God, that's all it took."

"Yes, ma'am." Jake gave her a warm smile. "I need to speak with him."

"I'm sorry, Detective, he's gone for the day. He's got a doctor's appointment this afternoon but should be back tomorrow."

"That's fine. It can wait." Jake closed his notebook. "Thanks for your time." He held the door for Mac. Time to find out what was bugging her.

But when they stepped into the hallway, she pivoted to face him. "I need to stay here a while longer." She placed a hand on his chest. "I have a few more things I want to look up. See you later at Sam's?"

"Sure." Jake kissed her on the cheek. "Don't be late." He rubbed his forehead and watched her walk away.

If he thought she'd listen to him, he'd insist Mac leave with him now. Seemingly simple occurrences had a way of getting complicated when she was involved, and he had a feeling this could be one of those times. But it was apparent she was on a mission, and he might as well keep his mouth shut. For now.

MACKENZIE ENTERED the windowless research room to find all her papers as she'd left them. A picture taken at the Easter parade in 2015 lay on top. She moved it to another spot on the table, smoothed the wrinkles out, and took several photos of it with her phone.

Her parents could be seen in the background speaking with a man. From their body language, the conversation seemed heated. If only she could make out who he was. It wasn't long after this photo was taken that they had their "accident." The accident that wasn't an accident at all.

Setting the picture aside, she picked up the phone book from that year. The good citizens of Washington, Missouri, still liked the White Pages back then, which made it a lot easier to find out who was living there. She thumbed to the U section and found an entry for Thomas Underwood and one other Underwood family member. Probably his parents. No Francis. She may have lived in another city, or if she was still living at home, her phone number would be the same as her parents'.

Douglas James was in there, but there was no way to tell if

he was married to Laura or not. Mac didn't remember her back then, but Mac wasn't around much. She'd have to ask her sister, Beth.

Mac closed the book and straightened the papers. Mrs. White preferred returning the files and photos to the stacks herself, so she left everything on the table. The name Underwood pestered her thoughts like a fly buzzing around her head. Time to call her sister and get some answers.

But contacting Beth would have to wait. Tonight, she had other plans. She and Jake were having dinner with her partner and her husband, Samantha and Alan Majors, at their house. Mac glanced at the clock and stuffed her notes into her bag. She'd have just enough time to go home and change.

"See you soon." She waved to Mrs. White as she passed her door on the way out.

"Goodnight, Mackenzie," the older woman said. "Be careful. It's raining."

Mac huddled under the awning, glaring out at the sheet of water pouring out of the sky. She pulled her sweater around her bag and sprinted to her car. Before jumping inside, she spied a sheet of paper plastered to the windshield. It was too miserable to spend time retrieving it. Besides, the message would be long gone anyway.

Tucked into the driver's seat, her bag on the passenger seat, and the car heater cranked up full blast, Mac raised her gaze to the windshield. Three words appeared as the defroster did its job.

*FORGET THE PAST.*

# CHAPTER 3

Mac leaped from the car and peeled the note off the windshield. Raindrops pelted her like tiny daggers hurled from the clouds. She dove back inside, slammed the door, and grabbed a plastic grocery bag from the back seat. After smoothing it out on the passenger side floor, she placed the sheet of paper on top to dry.

This wasn't the first time she'd received a threat like this, and it probably wouldn't be the last. She pushed aside the seed of anxiety before it grew into a field of fears—choosing instead to see it as a positive. She must be making someone nervous.

Now to share her news with Jake and Sam. She'd head straight over to Sam and Alan's place. She looked in the rearview mirror and groaned. Good thing they loved her for better or for worse, because this was one of her worst. She yanked a tissue from her purse and scrubbed black streaks of mascara off her cheeks before adding it to the pile stuffed in the driver's side door pocket.

Jake must have been watching for her arrival because as

soon as she pulled into Sam's gravel driveway, he came out the front door with an umbrella.

He shielded the open door from the rain while Mac gathered her things. "Where you been?"

"I'll tell you inside." She huddled next to him, slammed the door, and locked her car. "Thanks—"

He smothered her words with a kiss. "Come on." He hooked his arm around her waist, and they hustled up the sidewalk to the covered porch where Alan held the door for them.

Just inside, Sam handed her a thick bath towel. "You look like you could use this. Let me take your coat."

Mac stopped rubbing her hair and looked around. "Where's the pooch?"

"He's in his kennel."

"What'd he do?" Jake asked.

"Nothing. We're getting him used to it for when the baby comes." Alan led the way back to the kitchen-family room. "I'll let him out in a few minutes."

"Are you afraid he'll bite the baby?" Mac tossed the towel in the laundry room. "I can't imagine Killer hurting anyone, much less a baby."

"No. Not on purpose, but he's such a big lug." Alan lifted the lid on a pot simmering on the stove.

The aromas of garlic and onion drifted through the room, and her stomach growled. "What are you making?" She took an involuntary step forward.

"Spaghetti. I'm trying a new sauce recipe."

"If it tastes half as good as it smells, it's a keeper," Jake said.

Killer shot through the doorway from the hall and rose on his hind legs in front of Jake, front paws reaching for Jake's shoulders. The dog was almost as tall as the man. "Hello, big guy." Jake managed to stroke the wavy hair of the golden doodle's back while dodging doggy kisses.

After a few minutes, the doodle dropped to all fours and bounded over to Mac with his welcoming grin that always made him sneeze.

"Bless you." She sat in a chair and the dog plopped down beside her, tongue hanging out, his sturdy body leaning against her leg. She wrapped her arms around the dog's neck. "So good to see you." And she meant it. This sweet dog had almost lost his life trying to protect Sam, her best friend and partner. He would always be special to her.

Sam stood in the doorway, hands on hips, her belly swollen and her face a picture of perfect contentment. A brief pang of despair and jealousy took Mac by surprise. She was engaged to Jake. Within a year, they would be married, and if they wanted, they could start a family too. So, what was the problem?

"Everybody ready to eat?" Alan brandished a spoon.

"You bet." Jake took a seat next to her.

"Killer. Go to your bed." Sam pointed into the family room and then pulled out a chair across from Mac.

The dog trotted away. Wow. She already had the mom voice down.

Alan placed steaming bowls of noodles and sauce on the table along with a plate of garlic toast before taking a seat himself. The friends joined hands and Alan blessed the meal. For a time, the only thing heard was the clatter of utensils on china as everyone filled their plates.

"Delicious." Jake managed to say between bites.

Mac nodded.

"What I want to know is why you came in looking like a drowned ... kitten?" Alan asked.

"Good save, Alan." Mac glared at him and placed her fork

on her plate. "I'll show you." She left the table and returned with the note. "Have you got a large zipper baggie I can have?"

Alan rose and went to the pantry. "Will this do?"

"Perfect." Mac slipped the wrinkled note inside the baggie and pressed as much of the air out as she could before zipping it shut. "I found this on my windshield when I came out of the museum today."

Jake took it from her and held it up to the light. "What does it say?"

"'Forget the past.'"

Sam uttered a sharp intake of breath. Mac locked eyes with her partner.

"What does it mean?" Jake used his police officer voice. He was upset.

"I've been researching the death of my parents. That's why I was at the history museum today." She inclined her head toward the paper. "I think the note means I'm making progress."

"I thought your parents' death was an accident."

Mac shook her head. "It was meant to look that way. But the car didn't go over the bridge like it was supposed to." She met his eyes. "Chief Baker was there. He knows what happened."

Jake pushed his chair away from her as if to distance himself from her words. "I can't believe the Chief would cover up a murder."

"At the time, my sister, Beth, thought it was the Mob, and she and the Chief were afraid for the rest of us. So, they played it as an accident." Mac massaged her right temple. "But we found out the Mob had nothing to do with their deaths. Now I want to find out who really killed them."

"Only it sounds like somebody doesn't want you digging up old dirt."

"Maybe that's because some of it might stick to them."

# CHAPTER 4

Jake turned the baggie over in his hands. He didn't hold out much hope of getting any prints or DNA off the paper, but he'd send it through the lab anyway. "I'll have this processed tomorrow and follow you home tonight."

"Fine, but first we help with clean-up." Mac took off her sweater and rolled up her sleeves.

While the others put leftovers away, he grabbed the spaghetti pot and filled it with hot, soapy water. The methodical up-and-down motion as he scrubbed the sides lulled him, and he let his mind wander. Should he talk to the Chief about Mac's parents' deaths? Did they still have the file? The evidence—if any—that was collected?

"I think that one's clean, bro." Sam placed a gentle hand on his back. "I can take it from here. Why don't you go home? I'll see you tomorrow."

"Sorry. I wasn't much help." Jake rinsed his soapy hands and dried them before turning to hug his sister. "Thanks for a great dinner."

"It was all Alan." Sam glanced over her shoulder. "He's amazing."

Jake nodded, a sudden lump of emotion in his throat. "Tomorrow." He maneuvered past the kitchen table to where Mac and Alan stood. "I'm ready when you are." He gave Mac a quick smile and clapped Alan on the back. "Thanks, Alan. The meal was great."

"Anytime. You guys are always welcome."

Killer blocked the front door, his tail wagging.

Jake stooped in front of the big dog. "We wouldn't leave without saying goodbye to our favorite pooch." He ruffled the doodle's ears.

Mac stroked the soft hair on Killer's head. "See you later, sweetheart."

Sweetheart. Jake had a sudden desire to sweep her into his arms and go wake a judge to marry them right away. Not only because he loved her, but because he'd know she was safe— and he could get some much-needed sleep at night.

At her car, he pulled her in for a hug. "I'll sleep on the sofa tonight."

"Don't be silly." She scrunched her face at him. "It was one stupid note. I've had worse."

That much was true. He took her left hand in his and played with her ring finger. But things were different now. They had plans for a future together, something he'd prayed would happen for a long time. He raised his eyes to hers.

She must have read his need. "On second thought, I would feel better if you spent the night on the sofa." She caressed his cheek. "At least tonight."

He kissed her softly. "Let's go."

Jake stayed back just enough so that his headlights didn't blind her in her rearview mirror. He only had to run one of the two traffic lights on the way, but there was no one else at the intersection, and he was a police officer after all.

As they approached her house, he noticed a sedan parked on the street in front. Mac pulled into her driveway, and a man got out of the driver's side of the strange car. Nathaniel Xander Westcott III lifted his arm against the glare of Jake's headlights. What was he doing here? Jake swung in behind Mac and flung his door open.

"I thought you were in prison." Jake marched in Nate's direction.

"They let me out for helping them get to the big bosses." Nate stopped, but stood his ground.

"That doesn't explain why you're at Mac's house." Jake clenched and unclenched his fists as waves of rage and jealousy beat against his wall of control.

"I came to apologize to Mackenzie." Nate nodded at Mac, who stood next to Jake.

She placed a hand on Jake's arm. "It's okay. I knew he was getting out. He's living with Miss P."

Jake turned on her. "Why didn't you tell me?"

"I haven't had a chance." She cut her eyes to Nate. "And Miss P wasn't sure whether she was going to let him come back."

"Actually ..." Nate scratched his nose. "She didn't. I'm staying in a halfway house in Herman. I got special permission to visit you tonight."

Jake and Mac looked at him.

"It's not a sober-recovery house." He held up a hand. "I don't have a drug or alcohol problem. I just need a place to live for three years where they can keep track of me." He ducked his head. "And Aunt Prudence wouldn't have me. Not that I blame her."

Jake pushed aside a twinge of compassion. The man had known all along the danger Mac was in and said nothing. He'd allowed her to be kidnapped. A simple apology wouldn't square that in his book. "If you expect us to feel sorry for you, we—"

Mac squeezed his arm. "It cost him a lot to come here. Let him say what he came to say."

"Thank you." Nate squared his shoulders and looked Mac in the eye. "I'm sorry."

Jake uttered a rude noise, and Mac elbowed him in the ribs.

"I know there's no way I can ever recompense you for the hurt I caused." Nate slumped, and his eyes glistened with tears. "I'll have to live with what I did for the rest of my life. But if there is anything—anyway—I can help you in the future, please call me. My license to practice law has been revoked, but that doesn't mean I've lost all my knowledge or my contacts."

"Contacts?" Jake threw an arm in the air. "Like with the Mob? Look what good those did her before."

Nate backed up a few steps. "I meant other contacts." He glanced at Mac. "Call if you need me. My aunt knows how to get in touch." He turned and hurried to his car.

"Don't hold your breath waiting for the phone to ring," Jake yelled as Nate turned the corner.

The man got under his skin more than any other human being on the planet. Not just because Nate and Mac dated in college, although that was a big part of it. What had Mac seen in him? But there was something else. Something he couldn't put his finger on.

"Come inside, you big lug." Mac threaded her arm through his. "The neighbors will be calling the police—if they haven't already. What's gotten into you?"

Jake glanced around and shook his head. Ever since they got engaged, he struggled with these swings in his disposition.

One minute, he was an in-charge police detective—the next, he was a raving maniac. Was this normal?

"You sit." Mac removed her jacket. "I'll make us some peppermint tea."

"Later." He pulled her into his arms. "We need to talk."

Anxiety filled her amber eyes.

"Nothing's wrong." He brushed a honey-colored strand of hair behind her ear. "Mac, let's get married."

She giggled and backed away. "We are, silly."

"No. I mean tomorrow." He took her hands in his. "The wait is driving me nuts. I mean it. You've seen how I've been acting."

"We can't." She squeezed his hands. "You know that. There are too many people to consider. Like your mom in Florida and my sisters in Kansas City."

"We can get married and have a second ceremony later." Why not? That sounded perfectly reasonable to him.

Mac withdrew her hands. "I only want to say my vows before God in a church, not in some lawyer's office or at the courthouse." She raised her index finger. "And I only want to do it once."

"Okay." He should have known she'd feel that way. "But we need to set a date. And it has to be soon."

"Yes, boss." She grinned at him.

Boss. Only if she let him, but that was okay. He reached for her again, releasing her hair so it cascaded to her shoulders. Her moist lips parted as if expecting his kiss, and her amber eyes darkened with emotion. His heart pounded in his chest. "Mackenzie." He pressed his lips to hers, and her lithe body melted against him.

He needed to stop what was happening before it went too far. Before they did something they would regret later. But how, when her desire seemed to match his own? And did it really matter? They were practically married after all. He knew the answer, and he was summoning the strength to release her when the doorbell rang.

"Were you expecting someone?" His body and mind switched from passion to defense mode in a split second. He glanced at his gun lying on the table behind Mac.

# CHAPTER 5

Jake's arms hardened under her hands. Mac shook her head and put a finger to her lips.

"Mackenzie, I know you're in there. Open the door."

Mac and Jake sprang apart.

"Miss P." Her stomach knotted. "How did she know we ...?"

"She's got the gift." Jake ran a hand through his hair and straightened his shirt. "Like Sam."

Mac pulled her hair into a ponytail with shaking hands. "Do I look okay?" Her lips still felt puffy from all their kissing. Why did she feel like she had when her dad caught her and her first boyfriend necking on the porch? She was a grown woman, an engaged woman.

Jake grabbed a tissue and wiped mascara from under her eyes. "You'll do. Better answer the door."

"Miss P. Good to see you. What brings you here?" She worked to make her voice light and welcoming.

The tall, thin, gray-haired woman strode into the room and set her small suitcase down next to the sofa. "I heard about the threatening note on your car, and I've come to stay with you."

"Thank you, but that wasn't necessary." Mac smiled and gestured at her fiancé. "Jake offered to stay on the couch tonight."

"I surmised that would be the case." Miss P ran an appraising eye over them both. "That's why I'm here. It's very unseemly for a woman and her fiancé to stay alone in the same house. You need a chaperone." She folded her hands in front of her.

Mac shared a knowing look with Jake. Miss P was right. They did need a chaperone.

"Detective Sanders, I'm glad you're here. Don't get me wrong, but at the same time, Mac is like a daughter to me, and I feel the need to look out for her best interests."

"I understand, Miss P, and it's good to know she has you on her side." Jake picked up her luggage. "Let me help you with your things."

Tears stung the backs of Mac's eyes. What did she do to deserve the love of two such people? A blessing for sure. "I'll make us some tea."

"Excellent idea." Miss P followed Jake down the hall. "I won't be long."

And she wasn't. She returned to the kitchen within five minutes, dragging a bemused Jake behind her. Mac flashed him a questioning look.

"Detective Sanders tells me you two have been discussing wedding dates." Miss P lowered herself into the chair Jake pulled out from the table for her. "Thank you." She smiled at him. "For what it's worth, I believe you should get married as soon as possible. Don't mess about."

"Why do you say that?" So, while she was making tea, Jake was baring his soul to Miss P. Persuading her to help Mac see reason. She glared at her fiancé.

Jake gave her an innocent look over Miss P's shoulder.

"I know that things can happen in a heartbeat, and I don't want to see you regret waiting until it's too late."

A cold chill passed over Mac. "Don't talk like that. Nothing's going to happen, but we are planning to marry as soon as possible. We need to get his mom and my sisters here."

"No, you don't. Get married and set another time for a reception of sorts."

"But they would want to see us exchange vows, and I only want to do that once. In a church before God."

"Your obstinacy, my dear, may cause you great pain."

Mac placed a mug of tea before Miss P and one in front of Jake. She carried hers to the front window. *Lord, help me know what to do. You sent me Miss P for a reason. Is she speaking the truth?*

She returned to the table. "Let me run this by my sisters. And Jake, talk to your mom."

"Okay." He smiled at her. "Sounds like a plan."

Miss P settled into her chair. "Now, tell me about the message on your windshield."

Mac took a sip of her tea. "You know I went to the historic museum to start researching my parents' deaths."

"Did you find anything useful?"

"Maybe. There were some photos from the time, and documents from the store." Mac's brow furrowed. "Then Doug James, the electrician, was electrocuted."

"I heard about that." Miss P set her mug on the table. "Douglas always paid strict attention to detail in chemistry class. I can't imagine how he could have made such a mistake at a job he has been doing for almost twenty years."

"My feelings exactly." Mac nodded. "But it's his partner that has me puzzled. His name's Thomas Underwood, and I know I've heard that name before. I just can't remember where."

"You have, my dear." Miss P cocked her head at Mac. "Quinton Underwood, Thomas's father, was the accountant for your parents' business."

"Of course." A tingle of satisfaction ran through her—the satisfaction of having a space in her memory filled in. But then came another memory. She looked at Miss P. "Do you remember Mom and Dad having any issues with him?"

"I'm not sure. Let me think about that."

She had another idea. "Take a look at this photo. Is this Underwood?" She pulled up the photo on her phone of her parents at the Easter parade, arguing with a man in the background.

"It's rather blurry, but I believe that may be him." Miss P squinted at the small screen.

"Let me get my computer. Maybe I can make it clearer." Mac hurried to her office. When she got back, she displayed the cropped photo on the bigger screen.

"That's much better." Miss P pointed to the image. "I can see now that he isn't Quinton Underwood, but Oliver DeLuca, the restaurant owner next door."

"You're sure?" Her spirits sank like a stone in a puddle.

"Quite sure. Your parents had an ongoing battle with him about rats." Miss P dropped her voice to a conspiratorial level even though it was just Mac, Jake, and her in the house. "You see, he didn't keep his establishment as clean as he should, and the vermin would go next door into your parents' store as well. Your mother and father placed frequent calls to the health department, but to no avail."

"And Mr. DeLuca found out it was them who made the calls?"

"They made no secret of it." Miss P straightened. "Which I strongly advised against, but they were honest people."

"What did DeLuca do?" Jake asked.

"He threatened them, of course, but nothing ever came of it." Miss P nodded toward the image on the screen. "There were screaming matches on the street like those."

"When they were killed, was DeLuca a suspect?" Jake leaned forward.

"I wouldn't know. The Chief ruled it an accident." Miss P sighed. "I believe since they were in witness protection, and the girls were still around, he wanted to keep it quiet for their sake." She raised her eyes to Jake. "I suppose you could get the original file on the 'accident?'"

She made air quotes.

Jake squirmed in his chair. "I could try."

Miss P switched her gaze back to Mac. "I take it the note was on your windshield when you left the historic museum?"

"Yes. It was raining, and I thought it was a flyer." Mac rubbed her arm. "Until I got in and saw the message through the glass. 'Forget the past.'"

"And you took it to mean your investigation into your parents' murder."

"Wouldn't you?"

"Yes." Miss P took another sip. "It appears we now have two intentional accidents to investigate."

"Two?" Jake paused on his way to the sink.

"You don't think Douglas's electrocution this morning was an accident, do you?" Miss P raised her eyebrows at them.

# CHAPTER 6

Doug's electrocution was intentional? Mac had known it in her core but refused to acknowledge it before now. The question remained—how to prove it?

"I'll talk to the maintenance man tomorrow." Jake yawned and rubbed his eyes. "See what he has to say."

"Do you think someone tampered with the circuit breakers?" Mac asked. "Would he be able to tell if that happened?"

Jake shrugged. "I'll find out." He pushed off the counter. "It's been a long day. Can you get me a pillow and blanket?"

Mac hopped up and left the kitchen. The events of the day streamed across her mind like a black-and-white movie in fast forward as she gathered what Jake needed. He may be tired, but she doubted she'd sleep at all. "Here you are."

He plopped the bedding onto the sofa and tugged her closer until he could get both arms around her. "Stop thinking about what happened. You need to sleep."

Had he read her mind too? First Sam, then Miss P, and now

Jake. Where could she go for a little privacy if not in her own thoughts? "I ... how ...?"

"Your eyes had that look they get when you're off somewhere else."

She relaxed. He wasn't reading her mind after all. It was her eyes that gave her away. She'd have to work on that.

"Relax." He rubbed his hands down her back. "It'll all be there tomorrow." He kissed her cheek and trailed his lips across her face to her mouth.

Electricity coursed through her veins. Relax? But he did take her mind off everything else.

"Time for bed, you two." Miss P stood in the hallway, every inch the chaperone once more.

"Yes, ma'am." Jake dropped his arms and smiled at Mac. "Sweet dreams."

"You too." She turned and headed for her bedroom.


"Oof." Mac rolled over and fell out of bed with a crash. She lay, face pressed to the rug for a moment, assessing whether anything was bruised. Beyond her pride.

"Mackenzie, are you all right?" A knock at the door. "Are you hurt?"

She pushed to her feet. "I'm fine." No pain, so she guessed it was true.

Miss P cracked the door. "Are you sure? It sounded like you fell out of bed."

"I did." Mac threw her a smile. "But I'm okay."

"Oh dear." The older woman entered the room and came closer.

Mac remained still as Miss P surveyed her from the top of

her disheveled head of hair to her unpainted toenails. It was the only way she would believe that Mac was telling the truth.

Satisfied, she straightened. "Breakfast is ready. Get dressed and I'll meet you in the kitchen."

"What about Jake?"

"Detective Sanders was called away early this morning, my dear. He said he would catch up with you later."

Mac furrowed her brow. What could have been so urgent that Jake had to leave early? Had something new happened? Or was it to do with Doug's death? She yanked a pair of jeans off their hanger and threw them on the bed along with a long-sleeved T-shirt. A quick shower first.

Clean and dressed, Mac entered the kitchen to find Miss P on the phone. Her friend glanced at her, and for the first time that Mac could remember, she saw an expression akin to guilt on her face.

"I will think about it. That's all I will say right now." Miss P pressed End and slipped the phone into her pocket. "I have the eggs and bacon in the warming drawer." She bent to lift the plate and placed it before Mac.

"What is it?" Mac put a hand on her arm. "I know that phone call upset you."

Miss P stilled. "That was Nathaniel." She withdrew her arm. "He's asking to come stay with me." She turned to Mac, the lines on her face telling the story of her torn feelings. "He vows he's changed, and told me he came here to apologize to you."

"He did." Mac indicated for her friend to sit. "I think you should give him a chance. He's your only living relative. Your sister's son." She stretched her hand toward Miss P. "It doesn't change anything between us."

"Thank you, my dear." Relief smoothed the worry on her

friend's face. "But at the first sign of trouble, out he goes. I will make that very clear to him."

Mac squeezed Miss P's arm and picked up her fork. She prayed she hadn't made a big mistake. Jake's angry face from the day before popped into her mind, and her stomach soured. "I think maybe I'll just have some toast this morning."

"Are you ill?" Miss P placed a hand against her forehead and cheek.

"No." Mac gave her a warm smile. "I had a big dinner last night at Sam's and I'm just not hungry. Let's get ready and go to the office."

Half an hour later, Mac turned into the driveway at the corner of Second and Johnson Street behind Miss P's late-model sedan. "I think we beat Sam here."

"I believe we have." Miss P took Mac's arm and climbed the steps to the front porch.

"Hello." A voice came from the shadows.

Mac jumped in front of Miss P. "Who's there?"

"I didn't mean to frighten you." A woman clumped forward into a patch of sunlight. Her bent form leaned heavily on an ornately carved walking stick. As she raised her face, clear blue eyes gave Mac a piercing look. "I take it you're Mackenzie Love."

"I am, and this is Miss Prudence Freebody."

"I want to hire you." The woman pulled a wallet out of the pocket of her coat.

"Why don't we go inside where we can talk?" Miss P unlocked the door and ushered everyone through to the reception area. "I'll make us some coffee."

"I prefer tea."

"Tea it is, Miss ...?"

"Mrs. Ursula Green. I'm Douglas James's aunt on his mother's side."

Mac grabbed a yellow pad and a pencil and settled across from Mrs. Green. "I was there when Douglas was electrocuted."

"I know. That's why I'm here." She grimaced. "Would you mind if we sat at the table? I prefer harder chairs. Support for my back, you see."

"Sure." Mac reached to help her rise, but the woman waved her away.

Instead, Ursula Green grabbed her stick with both hands and pulled herself upright—as upright as her bent spine would allow. Mac pulled out a chair for the woman and took her usual spot. She made notes on her pad as Mrs. Green made her painful progress across the floor.

"Here you are." Miss P set a mug of steaming liquid before Mrs. Green. "I took the liberty of using a blend of turmeric and ginger, which are both excellent for inflammation."

"Thank you. A superb choice." The woman's smile transformed her face, and a hint of her youthful beauty appeared for an instant.

"Now, what can we do for you?"

"My nephew's electrocution was not an accident." She took a sip and set her mug down. "I want to hire you to find out who tried to kill him."

Mac studied the woman to her right. "How did you know I was on the scene?"

"I spoke to both his wife and his partner." She curled her lip. "What a pair they make. I wouldn't put it past either one of them to have figured out how to make it look like an accident."

Mac shared a look with Miss P over the woman's bent head.

"Why are you so sure it wasn't an accident?" Would Ursula Green have something more concrete than that Doug was meticulous and had been on the job for twenty years?

"He told Laura he wanted a divorce." Green's penetrating gaze met Mac's.

Mac shot her a questioning look.

The woman leaned forward. "Laura's response was ... over *his* dead body."

# CHAPTER 7

"Mrs. Green. Let me get this straight. You want to hire us to prove that Laura James tried to kill your nephew?" Mac stopped writing and stared at the woman across from her.

"Yes. And no. I realize that sounds near impossible, but if you can at least convince the police it wasn't an accident, maybe they'll pay attention to me." She threw up her hands. "Because they sure won't now."

Mac nodded. "I happen to agree with you. I can't see Doug making that big of a mistake. He was too good at his job."

"So you'll help me?"

"Yes. We'll look for evidence that Doug's accident wasn't an accident."

"Thank you." She pulled her wallet out once more. "How much do I owe?"

"Sam's our finance person—"

"Good morning, one and all." A smiling blonde, leading with her baby belly, entered with her usual cheerfulness. "What have I missed?"

Mac stood. "Sam, we have a new client. Mrs. Ursula Green. She's Douglas James's aunt, and she's hired us to prove that Doug's electrocution was intentional."

"How do you do. I'm Samantha Majors." She shook Ursula's hand. "I'm so sorry about what happened to Doug."

Leave it to Sam to say the one thing none of the rest of them had thought to.

"Thank you." Ursula's eyes softened. "He is my favorite nephew. This has been terrible." She sighed. "I'm glad you and your friends will help me set this right. I'm told you're the finance person of the group. What do I owe you?"

Sam raised her eyebrows at Mac. "Our rate varies per case based on difficulty." Sam gave the woman her sunniest smile. "Why don't I talk to you in a day or two to establish a payment schedule? Just leave your information so we can get in touch with you."

"That sounds reasonable. Do you have paper and a pen?"

After Ursula finished writing, the women went with her onto the front porch to wait for her ride.

"We'll talk soon." Mac closed the taxi door and stepped back onto the curb. Yet again, she and Jake were officially working on the same case. Time to call him and let him know. She trudged back to the porch.

A car pulled into the drive, and a woman hopped out. "Sorry I'm late. David's car wouldn't start, and I had to give him a ride to his studio." She strode up the lawn to where Mac waited on the porch. "Was that a client?" She waved a hand toward the taxi.

"It was." Mac folded her arms across her chest. "Glad to see you could make it, Zoe." She pivoted and pushed the door open. "Come on in and we'll tell you all about it."

"Great."

Sarcasm was totally lost on this woman. Mac shook her head.

"Ms. Dixon, where have you been?" Miss P stood ramrod straight with her hands folded in front of her.

Zoe's confident step faltered.

Ouch. Mac almost felt sorry for her old classmate.

"I'm sorry, Miss P. David's car wouldn't start, and I had to give him a ride to his studio."

"And you couldn't give us a call because ...?" The former chemistry teacher peered at the younger woman over her glasses.

"I ... um ... I didn't think about it?" Zoe shrugged one of her well-formed shoulders and offered a weak smile.

"Next time, think about it, young lady." Miss P spun on her heel. "Now. We have a new client. Take a seat at the conference table."

"Yes, ma'am." She hung her jacket on the back of a chair and sat.

Miss P placed a fresh pad of paper and a pencil in front of her, along with a cup of tea.

"Zoe, you changed your hair." Sam cocked her head.

"Do you like it?" She fluffed the auburn waves that cascaded around her shoulders. "I thought the blonde color made me look too much like an airhead. Now that I'm working for you guys, I need to look more professional." She pulled it back into a thick ponytail.

Mac sighed to herself. Sam, with her shining blonde hair, sat across from Zoe, and she was one of the most intelligent, skilled women Mac knew. There was more to being professional than hair color.

"So." Zoe smiled brightly at each of them. "What did I miss?"

After filling her in, Mac tapped her pencil against her notes.

"We're going to need to interview his wife, Laura, his partner, Thomas Underwood, and the maintenance man at the historic museum to begin with."

"I believe Detective Sanders said he would be speaking to the maintenance man today." Miss P picked up the phone. "Shall I call him?"

"No." Mac stood. "I'll do it. See what you can find on Laura and Underwood. We'll see about speaking to them after I get back."

She crossed to her office and shut the door. When she and Sam bought the house, Sam insisted Mac use the bedroom at the front. It was a generous offer. One Mac was thankful for every day. With windows on two sides, the room was filled with light. The green walls and oak furniture—most of it antique—calmed her and helped her think.

She plopped into her comfortable desk chair and dialed Jake's number.

"Morning, sweetheart. Sorry to cut out so early." The sound of rustling papers came over the phone, followed by another voice.

"You sound busy. Maybe you could call me back."

"No, it's fine." A wariness crept into his voice. "What's up?"

"I was wondering if I could tag along when you talk to the maintenance man today."

"Why?" He dragged the word out.

She rubbed between her eyes where a headache threatened to form. "Because we've been hired by Doug's aunt to prove his electrocution wasn't an accident."

"Doug's aunt? Why don't I know about this aunt?"

"I don't think she's been to the police yet."

"Why not?" Jake's voice took on a strident tone.

"She seems to think the police won't listen to her until she has some proof. That's where we come in." Mac matched Jake's tone with a calming one. "Jake, please. She's worried and confused. She doesn't know you like I do. Let me ride along with you to the interview."

He heaved a sigh. "Be here at eleven."

"I love you."

"Love you more."

The line went dead before she had a chance to tell him about Nate staying with Miss P.

# CHAPTER 8

Mac swung her car into a space at the Public Safety Building at the corner of Fourth Street and Jefferson. The police department took up the second floor while other government offices filled the first. She waited outside and texted Jake to let him know she was there.

Five minutes later, he pushed the glass door open and ushered a woman with long black hair through before him. Laura James. What was she doing here? They stopped on the sidewalk for a moment, and then the woman gave Mac's fiancé a hug and a kiss on his cheek.

Laura trailed a hand down his arm as she moved away. Mac jumped out and glared daggers at the woman's back before turning them on Jake, who had the good sense to look sheepish. He hurried over and reached for her.

She avoided his embrace. "We need to get going." She beeped her car locked and strode toward his SUV.

Jake caught her arm and turned her to face him. "Now you know how I felt when Nate showed up at your house the other night. Except Laura was here on legitimate business."

"What business?" Mac put a hand on her hip.

"Her statement." He crossed his arms over his chest. "Which you have yet to do."

"Well ..." she glanced toward the door. "She shouldn't go around hugging and kissing on another woman's fiancé."

"You're right." He held his hands up in submission. "She caught me off guard, but I should have blocked it."

"Yes, you should have."

"I'll do better if it ever happens again." He kissed her and opened the car door for her.

Inside, Mac's curiosity got the better of her. "What did Laura have to say? Why was she at the historic museum that morning?"

"You know I shouldn't tell you that." He glanced at her.

"You're pulling that on me after all the times we've shared information?" She shifted in her seat so she could see his face. "Did she say something that would incriminate her? I mean, why can't you tell me what she said?"

"You have this thing about Laura."

"What thing? You mean because I think she's coming on to you?" The muscles in her jaw tightened. Was he questioning her judgment? He was the one with clouded judgment. "I will have you know that I am very capable of divorcing my private feelings about someone from my professional opinion."

Jake ran a hand down his face. "I didn't mean that exactly."

"Then what did you mean—exactly?" Her words dripped with sarcasm, and it occurred to her that they were having a fight.

"Nothing. Just forget it."

"Then tell me what she said."

"No."

What just happened? Jake always said they worked well together. She stole a look at his stony face. Was this the end of their collaboration? Dread formed a lump in her throat and made it hard for her to swallow. They rode the next few blocks in uneasy silence.

The SUV bumped over the curb into the parking lot at the historic museum. Jake shut the engine off and turned to Mac. "I'm sorry. I will tell you what Laura said, but let's do this interview first."

"I'm sorry too." Mac released her belt and grabbed his face between her hands. "Thank you." She kissed him and hopped out of the SUV before her tears had a chance to spill over and down her cheeks.

Jake took her hand as they walked toward the building. Mrs. White greeted them at the door.

"I'm so glad to see you both again." Mrs. White held her clasped hands in front of her. "I have Mr. Zane, our maintenance man, waiting in the conference room." She took off down the hall. "He's so nervous, poor man, and I don't blame him." She paused at the door. "He's certain he did something wrong, and you're here to arrest him." Her voice rose on the last two words.

"We need his help. That's all." Jake gave her a reassuring smile. "Would it help if you sat in on the interview?"

She glanced into the room and gave her head a quick shake. "No, I don't think so. I just wanted you to know before you spoke with him."

"It will be fine." Another smile, and Jake motioned for Mac to enter the room.

A wiry little man sat hunched over the far end of the table. When he lifted his head, brilliant aquamarine eyes shone from under thick black lashes in a face made up of angles. The sleeves of his blue work shirt were rolled up to the elbow and exposed a series of tattoos.

"Mr. Zane, I'm Detective Jake Sanders, and this is Private

Investigator Mackenzie Love. We're here to ask you a few questions about the day Douglas James was electrocuted." Jake pulled out a chair for Mac and sat next to her. "We need your help."

As Jake uttered the last words, Zane's posture relaxed. "I'll do what I can, but I wasn't here when it happened."

"We know." Jake ran his pen down a page in his notebook. "Mrs. White called you to come over and get the power back on."

Zane nodded.

"What time was that?"

"About ten."

"Can you walk us through what you did?" Jake stood.

"Sure." The man pushed away from the table and rubbed his hands on his canvas work pants. "We need to go to the electric panel."

"Lead the way."

Mac brought up the rear of their short parade through the historic museum. As they passed the copy room, her stomach churned. The wiring still dangled from the ceiling. Jake and Zane turned the corner, and when she caught up, Zane had opened a door at the end of the hall, revealing a large electrical panel.

"What happened when you opened the panel?" Jake asked.

"I examined the fuse for the copy room." Zane pointed to one about one-third down the left-hand side. "It was still on, but the one below it—the one for the conference room—was off."

"Don't touch anything." Jake grabbed Zane's hand. "You're saying this fuse was off, but this one was on."

"Yeah. I guess Doug got the wrong one."

Mac moved in closer. The fuses were marked with paste-on labels. "Could the labels have been switched?"

"Naw. They're hard to remove."

"How about the fuses?" Jake asked. "Would the fuse from the conference room work in the copy room and vice versa?"

Zane peered at them again. "Yeah. They're both the same size."

"We're going to need both those fuses. Do you have spares?"

"Yeah, but ..." Zane leaned against the doorframe and stared at Jake. "Are you thinking someone messed with the fuses? They'd need a key to get to the box."

"Don't get excited." Jake held up his hands. "This isn't Fort Knox. I'm sure if someone wanted in through this door, they could do it."

"Who has keys to the door?" Mac asked.

"Me and Mrs. White." Zane pulled out a chain filled with keys of all sorts. "Mine is always with me. I don't know where Mrs. White keeps hers."

"Mr. Zane, all I need you to do is get replacement fuses and let's make the switch so I can take these back to the lab for printing." Jake smiled at him. "We'll worry about the key thing later."

"Okay. Give me a minute."

After Zane left, Mac shined her flashlight on the fuse box. "What do you think?"

"Someone switched the fuses. Doug thought he was flipping the one for the copy room when he was turning off power to the conference room." Jake sighed. "Pretty devious."

"But getting shocked by household current doesn't come close to killing most people. Why did Doug's heart stop?" Mac turned to Jake.

"I don't know, but somebody did." He held her gaze. "He—or she—is lucky Doug didn't die, or they'd be looking at murder instead of attempted murder."

# CHAPTER 9

Mac looked at her watch. Zane had been gone twenty minutes, and something told her he wasn't coming back. "I think our maintenance man has done a runner."

Jake yanked his phone from his pocket. "I need a tech at the historic museum pronto. And an electrician."

"Do you think he switched the fuses?" Mac wrinkled her nose.

Jake finished putting out an APB on Zane and frowned at her. "You don't?"

She shrugged. "What would be his motive?"

"He wouldn't need a motive if he was working for someone else."

She hadn't thought of that. "If that's the case, he wouldn't have to be here. He could have switched the fuses any time before Doug came."

"Exactly."

An officer came around the corner with a man in a blue work shirt with Stone Electric over the pocket. "What do you need, Detective?"

"I want these two fuses replaced." Jake nodded at the electrician and handed him a pair of latex gloves. "You'll need to wear these." He pointed to the officer. "And you, bag and tag them for fingerprints."

"Got it." The officer pulled on his own pair of gloves.

"After that, print the rest of the box and the door."

The officer nodded.

"Let me know as soon as you've got anything." Jake backed away from the room.

"Will do."

"Let's find Mrs. White. I need her key." He placed his hand on Mac's back and guided her away from the electrical closet.

"Is everything okay?" Mrs. White met them in the hall. "I just saw Mr. Zane run out of here as if someone were chasing him."

"We need to speak with you in your office." Jake nodded in that direction.

"Certainly." The older woman gave Mac a worried look. "I hope it's nothing serious."

Mac took her arm as they walked. "It has to do with Douglas's electrocution. We may have found out what happened."

She turned mournful eyes on Mac. "It wasn't an accident, was it?"

"I'm afraid not."

"And Mr. Zane?" She paused at the door to her office.

"We have reason to believe he may have been involved." Jake opened the door and motioned them inside.

"Oh dear. He's such a kind man and a wonderful worker." Mrs. White sat behind her desk. "Are you sure?"

Her eyes begged Mac for an answer she couldn't give. "It looks like it." Mac reached for her friend's hand. "I'm sorry."

"I'm afraid I tend to think the best of people, as Mac can

attest to." Mrs. White straightened and pressed her lips together. "What can I do to help?"

"We need Zane's full name, address, and phone number for starters." Jake removed his notebook.

The historian settled her glasses on her nose and opened her computer. "His name is Zachary Zane." She wrinkled her brow. "He once told me his friends called him ZZ. It was supposed to be a joke, but I didn't understand what was so funny."

"There's a rock group named ZZ Top."

"I see." She did a slow nod and returned her attention to her computer screen. "His address is 301 W. Front Street." Her eyes widened. "That can't be right."

Jake stopped writing and heaved a sigh. "That's the train station. Give me his phone number."

She read it off. "I know that's correct because I call him all the time."

"Does he list any relatives?"

"We don't require that to work here." Mrs. White closed her computer. "I'm sorry, Detective. I haven't been of much assistance to you."

"No problem." He smiled at her. "What about his car? What was he driving?"

"I did notice that." Her face brightened. "He was in an old gray truck. The driver's door was blue."

"Good." Jake nodded as he wrote. "That helps."

"If you think of anything else, Mrs. White, you can call me or Jake." Mac stood, rounded the desk, and hugged her friend.

"I did find something else you might be interested in for your other search." Mrs. White withdrew a file and handed it to Mac. "These are copies of the notes from your parents' lawyer. I'm not sure why we have them, but I thought they might help you find what you're looking for."

Mac's stomach churned. With all the excitement around Doug's supposed accident, she'd forgotten for a time about her parents and what had brought her to the historic museum in the first place. "Thanks." She jammed the folder into her bag and turned to go. Her parents' case would have to wait.

Outside, Jake pulled his phone from his pocket and beeped the SUV open for her.

"Next of kin and last known address." Jake paused. "Driving an old gray truck with a blue driver's door. Got all that?" He tossed his phone on the console and pressed start.

"Where to next?" Mac clicked her belt.

"I'm taking you back to your car." He shifted into reverse.

"Excuse me?" Her hands tightened into fists. "And what are you going to do?"

"Police stuff." He cut a hard glance her way.

"What's with you? You used to take me with you. You said we worked well together. What happened to that?"

His jaw jutted forward. "We're engaged."

"So?"

"It's different, that's all."

"You're being stupid."

"So now I'm stupid?"

"No." She lowered her voice. "I didn't say you were stupid. I said what you're doing is ... stupid."

"What's the difference?"

"Okay." She sighed. "I'm sorry. That was a bad choice of words."

"I'll say it was." He bounced over the curb into the parking lot and stopped.

"Jake, please." She unbuckled and reached for him.

"I'll call you later." He kissed her on the cheek.

# CHAPTER 10

Mac slammed the front door at the offices of Mackenzie Love and Samantha Majors, Private Investigators. "I can't believe your brother." She yanked her coat off and threw it on the sofa. "He's so stu ... stubborn."

Sam smirked at her. "What's he done now?"

"He refuses to take me along with him on his investigation because we're engaged." Mac threw up her arms. "Does that make any sense at all?" Frustration boiled over into anger. "And, he promised to tell me what Laura James said in her statement—which he never did."

"That stinks," Zoe said. "How are we going to know anything?"

Miss P retrieved Mac's jacket and hung it on the coat rack. "It sounds to me as if Detective Sanders is still working out what his role should be as an engaged man."

"Why should it be any different than it was before?" Mac plopped into a chair at the table in the middle of the long room that served as both reception and consultation areas. "At least on the professional side of things."

"Apparently, he's having some trouble separating the personal from the professional." Miss P sat and pulled two file folders from a stack to her right.

"What do you think, Sam?"

"I'm staying out of it." She grinned at Mac. "My brother and my best friend? That's a no-win situation."

"You used to have something to say."

"Yeah, but you weren't engaged then."

"If I hear that—"

"Excuse me." Miss P used her teacher voice. "I believe it would be best if we changed the subject. I have been doing some research on Laura James and Thomas Underwood." She passed sheets of paper across to Mac, Sam, and Zoe. "It appears Mrs. James was married before."

Mac scanned the sheet in her hand. "And her first husband died in an accident." She air-quoted the word accident. "Isn't that interesting? I wonder if Jake knows that?"

"I sent my findings on both Mrs. James and Mr. Underwood to Detective Sanders earlier today." Miss P removed her glasses and polished them with a special cloth she kept handy.

"She was so young." Compassion tinged Sam's voice.

Zoe sighed in commiseration. "And no kids."

"This poor woman may have tried to kill Doug." Mac scoffed. "And who's to say she didn't kill her first husband too?"

"You think we're dealing with a black widow?" Zoe's eyes widened.

"Ladies, let's not get ahead of ourselves." Miss P peered at them over her glasses. "We were hired to prove Douglas's electrocution was not an accident. We've done that."

"Not yet." Mac held up a finger. "We still have to prove

someone switched the fuses. Until then, it's only a theory—a good one, but still a theory."

"You *were* paying attention in class." Miss P gave her a rare smile of approval. "You make a good point. Until then, we should continue forward with our investigation. I suggest I research the untimely death of Mrs. James's first husband."

"I think it's time Zoe and I paid a visit to Laura James to offer our support." Mac pushed away from the table.

"Before you do, there's more to discuss." Miss P waved her back.

Mac let out a sigh. "What?"

"Don't sigh at me, young lady." Miss P gave her a stern look. "It has to do with insurance."

Mac pulled her notepad in front of her and prepared to write.

"It's on the sheet I gave you if you'd taken the time to read it more thoroughly."

She furrowed her brow as she read through the sheet more carefully this time. "Whoa." Laura James stood to gain five hundred thousand dollars and half interest in the company upon the death of her husband. "The problem for her is that the electrocution didn't kill Doug. He's in a coma."

"Turn it over." Miss P made a graceful motion with her hand.

"This has stuff about Underwood." Why would she need to know this before talking to Laura James?

"Read."

Mac ran her finger down the page as she read the background on Thomas Underwood. She stopped and pulled her hand away. "He has a one-million-dollar partner life insurance policy on Doug and first rights to buy the company." A picture of Laura greeting Underwood at the museum flashed into her mind. She'd told him Doug was dead. Was that a message? Were they in it together?

Zoe whistled. "That's a lot of money."

"That's a lot of *incentive*." Mac stood once more. "Thanks, Miss P." She turned to Zoe. "You ready to go?"

"Great." Zoe lifted her arms to adjust her ponytail. Her tight T-shirt stretched across her ample chest.

Mac groaned. "Speaking of looking professional, you're going to have to wear something different than those T-shirts. For now, leave your jacket on."

"What's the matter with what I'm wearing?" The auburn-haired woman looked down. "Oh. Got ya."

"Your car's in back so can you drive?" Mac pulled the front door shut behind them.

"Sure." Zoe led the way to her four-door sports vehicle.

They were the same age, but for some reason, Mac always felt older. Like she was the old dog with a new puppy. It couldn't have anything to do with life experience. Zoe had been through a lot, too, including a nasty divorce. Maybe it was because Mac always had a clear idea of what she wanted to do, and Zoe was just figuring it out.

"Where are we going?" Once buckled, Zoe turned to Mac.

"She lives in Holtgrewe Farms. Do you know where that is?"

"Yeah. My sister's mother-in-law lives there." Zoe hit the accelerator.

Mac grabbed the handle above the window and whispered a silent prayer.

Ten minutes later, Mac willed the muscles of her hand to open and slid out of the car.

"I like having you in the car," Zoe said. "When David rides with me, he sits over there and gasps the whole time."

"I wonder why." Mac didn't bother to keep the sarcasm out

of her voice while she flexed her right hand. "When we're inside, let me do the talking."

"Got it."

The house sat on an incline with the two-car garage built into the bottom level. Mac led the way up the steps to the front porch and rang the bell.

"My sister's mother-in-law lives about three houses that way." Zoe pointed farther down the street. "Boy, you can see a long way from up here."

Mac leaned on the bell again. She was ready and eager to speak to Laura, but as the minutes passed, frustration set in. The woman wasn't home. She glanced around. Was there anyone out she could ask about where Laura might be? "Do you think your sister's whoever might know Laura?"

"My sister's mother-in-law." Zoe narrowed her eyes. "She might. She is something of a busybody. Want to go talk to her?"

"It can't hurt."

A quarter of a mile down the street, Zoe pulled into a broad driveway. A lovely one-story home with a walk-out in the back. Flowers surrounded the mailbox. "This is it."

A gray-haired woman in slacks and a cotton blouse met them at the door with a broad smile. "Zoe. How nice to see you."

"We were in the neighborhood and thought we'd stop by." Zoe stepped aside. "This is my boss, Private Investigator Mackenzie Love."

"Nice to meet you." Mac shook the woman's soft hand.

"Come in and sit. Would you like something to drink?"

"I'll take a water," Zoe said.

"Coming right up."

Mac took in the room. A beautiful rug covered part of the wood floor between two sofas flanking the fireplace, a low oak table between them. Three old wooden boxes were stacked on the hearth next to a cast-iron bootjack. Every available surface held pottery, framed photos, or some other interesting item.

"Do you like it?"

Mac hadn't heard the woman return. "I love it. I'm an amateur antique collector."

"This took years." The woman patted her arm. "You'll get there one day." She sat on one of the couches. "Tell me what brings you to my neighborhood."

"We came to speak to Laura James. Do you know her by any chance?"

"Poor thing." Her eyes darkened with sympathy. "I heard about Doug."

"How well do you know Mrs. James?"

"We have a common interest." The woman waved her hand around the room. "She loves antiques as well. In fact, she works part-time in Hermann at one of the stores there. I forget which one."

"Do you think that might be where she is today?"

"Oh no. I expect she's at the hospital. With her husband."

Mac did a mental head slap. Of course. "Thank you for your time. Your house is lovely."

The woman rose. "Come back any time, Ms. Love." She hugged Zoe. "And you. You don't need an excuse to visit. I love seeing you."

"Love you too." Zoe waved as they walked back to the car. She grinned at Mac. "To the hospital?"

"No." Mac gazed out the window. "Confronting her in the hospital doesn't seem like a good idea. We need to speak to her in a more neutral setting." She turned to Zoe. "Let's see if we can find Thomas Underwood."

# CHAPTER 11

Why did he feel like such a jerk? Jake banged his hand against the steering wheel. If he let Mac come along, he'd be putting her in harm's way, but if he didn't, it was like he was shutting her out. What should he do? Things were different now that they were engaged. Weren't they? He looked upward and turned his questions into prayers. He glanced over at Detective Victor Young.

"So we're on our way to interview this Mrs. Xavier?"

"Yes. She's the sister of a suspect in the attempted murder of Douglas James." Jake stopped at a light. "Give me the address."

Vic read it out loud. "Doug's accident was intentional? I'm really behind."

"Mac and I went to the historic museum to speak to the maintenance man, Mr. Zane, this morning. Two fuses were switched before Doug got there yesterday. He thought he was turning off the power to the copy room, but it was the conference room."

"You think the maintenance man did it?"

"When I asked him to get new fuses so we could take the old ones away for fingerprinting, he left and never came back." Jake slowed for a stop sign. This trip didn't justify speeding through intersections.

"That's what the APB on Zane is about."

"Yes." Jake's radio came alive. A gray truck with a blue driver's door had been spotted at a residence. The address matched the one given for Zane's sister. Suddenly, time was of the essence. He hit the switch for lights and siren. Cars dove for the curb as he roared through the narrow streets of Washington.

The house stood on a corner lot, but the street on its side went back two hundred feet to woods. The suspect's truck was parked with its nose up against the trees. Jake pulled in behind the patrol car in front of the house.

"Have you seen anyone coming or going?" Jake asked the officer.

"No, sir."

"Okay. You wait here and keep an eye on the truck and the side of the house." Jake nodded at Vic and they crossed the pavement.

The house was a modest brick home with a two-car garage that faced the side street. The detectives took the sidewalk to the front porch, and Jake pointed out the entryway camera. He pressed the doorbell.

"Coming." The door opened with a swoosh. The heavy metal storm door remained closed. "What do you want?"

The woman's slight accent was hard to place. Italian? "I'm Detective Jake Sanders and this is Detective Victor Young. We're looking for Zachary Zane."

"He's not here."

"He was last seen driving that truck." Jake inclined his

head toward the side street. "So he's been here recently. May we come in and speak to you about where he is now?"

"No. Let me get my shoes. I will come out." She shut the door.

Last time this happened, the person never came back. Jake lifted his chin at Vic. "Walk around the side of the house. Make sure she doesn't try to take off."

A moment later, the dark-haired woman opened the storm door and stepped out onto the porch. "Where is your partner?"

"He's taking a look around." Jake put his fingers to his mouth and whistled.

Vic appeared soon after.

"Mrs. Xavier, we need to speak to your brother. It's important. If you're hiding him inside, you could end up in a lot of trouble." Jake gave her his sternest look.

"You don't scare me, Detective." She crossed her arms over her chest and glared at him. "I have dealt with your kind many times before."

Jake ran a hand through his hair and took a step back. He wouldn't get anywhere with this woman by antagonizing her. "Sorry." He held up his hands, palms out. "I didn't mean to come on so strong." He pressed his lips together in a grim smile. "We're concerned that your brother may have gotten himself mixed up with someone bad."

She rubbed her forehead with the fingers of her right hand. "It wouldn't be the first time."

"I know what it's like to love someone who's always making poor decisions and trusting the wrong people." He lowered the timbre of his voice.

She eyed him cautiously. "What do you want to know?"

"We know he was driving the truck parked around the corner. Did he get another vehicle?" Jake willed all the compassion he could into his gaze. "Or is he inside?"

"He drove off in my car." Tears flooded her dark eyes.

"What kind of car is it?" Jake asked softly.

"A Toyota Camry. Two thousand four. White." She began to sob. "He's a good man. Don't hurt him."

"Thank you." Jake put an arm around her shoulders. "I know that was hard." He turned to Vic. "Let's go."

Vic stopped him before they got into the SUV. "I looked in the garage through a window. The car she described was inside."

Jake glanced back at the house. "Check with the DMV to make sure they don't have two of the same make and model."

"I did. They don't." Vic adjusted his sunglasses. "Only the truck and the one Toyota."

Jake balled his hands into fists. The woman was good. He hadn't been taken in like that for a long time. Those had been real tears on her face. He took a step toward the house.

"Take it easy." Vic placed a hand on his arm. "If Zane's in there, he's more likely to show himself if we pretend to leave."

"Stay here." Jake pointed a finger at the officer. "Wait an hour and then leave as if you got another call."

"Yes, sir."

"Come on." Jake stomped over to his SUV. "How many ways out of here?"

"Just the one. The street circles back to the junction up the block."

"Good." A perfect ambush spot.

# CHAPTER 12

Mac hovered a finger over her speed dial. What was Jake doing now? Had he found Mr. Zane? Was he interrogating him? She'd sure like to be in on that one. But, nooo. Mr. "I'm your fiancé" didn't think it was a good idea for them to work together anymore. "Grrrrr."

"What?" Zoe asked.

"Nothing." Mac threw her phone into her bag. "I'm just venting."

"Oh."

"Here's our turn." Mac pointed to the right. "His office is supposed to be on the right." She peered out the window. "There it is."

Zoe jerked the little sports vehicle over to the curb. After five forward and backward adjustments, she seemed satisfied with her parking job and turned the car off.

Mac pried her hand off the handle and opened the door. Next time, she'd drive. She didn't care if they had to shuffle three cars in the driveway.

"Which way is it?" Zoe smiled at her.

Mac nodded to her right as she straightened her jacket and composed her nerves.

"What do we know about him?"

"He started out working for his father, doing accounts for other people. Then, he became friends with Doug and ended up buying into the company. That was about six years ago."

"Cool." Zoe's gaze swept over the entrance to the office. "Impressive."

A rich, dark green double door with gold lettering welcomed them in. Doug's electrical company was flourishing, but was it that prosperous? Or did Underwood still take other clients as well? The tinkle of a bell announced their entry.

"May I help you?" A woman with perfect make-up and hair gave them a no-nonsense smile from a desk to the left.

"I'm Private Investigator Mackenzie Love"—she displayed her credentials—"and this is my associate, Zoe Dixon. We'd like to speak to Thomas Underwood."

"Do you have an appointment?" The woman played her fingers over the keyboard of her computer and scanned the screen.

"No. I'm here to speak to him about Douglas James. I met him at the historic museum the day Mr. James was electrocuted."

The woman's smooth brow furrowed. "Let me see if he has a few minutes. Please take a seat." She rose and disappeared through a door behind her.

Zoe bounced on the chair. "We should get some like these."

"Sit still." Mac glared at her—although she'd been thinking the same thing. Elegant was the word she'd use to describe the space. Thick carpet, wood paneling, and a chandelier. Everything screamed money. But from part-ownership in an electrical business? Maybe he'd inherited. That could be. After all, she had.

"Mr. Underwood will see you." The woman narrowed her eyes at Mac. "But make it short. He's a very busy man."

Mac caught herself before she said something rude. "We will."

The inner office was somewhat of a letdown after the reception area. Still comfy chairs, but worn, and the carpet was thick, but older, and the lighting subdued. Underwood came around his scarred oak desk to greet the women.

"Ms. Love." He shook her hand. "And Ms. Dixon?" He offered Zoe a smile. "Please, make yourselves comfortable. What can I do for you?" He perched on the corner of his desk.

"My private investigation agency has been hired to look into the electrocution of Douglas James." Mac nodded at Zoe, who removed her notebook from her purse. "We'd like to ask you a few questions, if that's okay."

"May I ask who hired you?" Underwood rose and moved around to sit behind his desk.

"I can't tell you that." Mac threw him a brief smile.

He fiddled with some papers before raising his gaze to her. "What do you want to know?"

"How long have you been a partner in Doug's business?"

"A little over six years. I was his accountant before that."

"And how long was that?"

"Three—four years?"

"So you know him pretty well, wouldn't you say?"

"Yes, we've become friends through the years." He leaned his arms on the desk. "He's a great guy. I ..." He ran a hand down his face. "I keep hoping I'll get a call that he's started breathing on his own again."

"I know." Mac lowered her eyes. "We all do." She paused. "There's reason to believe his electrocution was no accident."

"What are you saying?" Underwood jolted upright.

"That someone tried to murder your friend." She held her breath as she studied the man across from her for his reaction.

"Who would want ..." He stilled as his tanned face paled and his brows knit together, shadowing his eyes. "What makes you think someone tried to kill Doug?"

"I'm not at liberty to say, but the evidence is compelling." She tracked him with her gaze as he jumped to his feet and paced behind his desk. "What aren't you telling us, Mr. Underwood?"

"It just took me by surprise. That's all." He sat and placed his folded hands on the desk.

"I think it's more than that. I think you have an idea of who might have done this to Doug." Mac let each word drop like a stone into a still pond and waited for the ripples to disturb the calm surface he was trying to maintain.

He raked a hand through his mane of gray hair. "I don't want to get anyone in trouble."

"Let me help you." Mac scooted forward on her chair. "In cases like this, the spouse is always the first one the police look at."

He raised his gaze to hers.

"Keep in mind, the burden of proof lies with the police. A person is innocent until proven guilty, and that includes Laura." His shoulders dropped an inch. "She was the first person who came to mind, wasn't she?"

Underwood gave a small nod.

Mac sat back. She should be asking more questions, but she didn't have the heart. The pain on the man's face pressed in on her, and all she wanted was to escape into the cool air. They could always come back another time. She signaled Zoe to close her notepad. "Thank you, Mr. Underwood. We've taken enough of your time." Mac stood and offered her hand.

"Of course, Ms. Love." He took her hand in his. "I want to help. Any way I can." He gave Zoe a little bow. "Ms. Dixon."

On the sidewalk, Zoe pulled her into a doorway. "Why didn't we ask him why he was at the historic museum? Or about the insurance?"

"You saw him." Mac pushed her face close to Zoe's. "He was devastated by the news that someone tried to kill Doug."

"Wouldn't that have been a good time to push him?"

"If you're such a crack investigator, you can take over next time." Mac stomped off.

"I didn't mean to make you mad. I was just asking." Zoe caught up with her. "Please. Come on, Mac." She jumped in front of her. "I'm sorry."

"So am I." Mac rubbed her forehead. "You're right. I should have asked him those questions when he was most vulnerable." She shook her head. "But I ... I just wanted out of there."

Zoe pulled Mac in for a big hug. "I get it."

Mac stiffened. Hugging another girl wasn't exactly her thing. Especially in the middle of the sidewalk. But, she had a feeling if she didn't hug Zoe back, the woman would keep her arms around her until she did. So she lifted her arms and gave Zoe a quick hug, and when she did, something happened that she didn't expect. She—Mac—began to cry.

# CHAPTER 13

Mac clung to Zoe and sobbed. What was wrong with her? She couldn't seem to stop. Somehow she knew it had to do with Jake, but she wasn't sure how. He wasn't even there.

"Let it all out." Zoe patted her back. "You'll feel much better."

Mac drew in a shuddering breath. "I'm finished." She dug in her purse for some tissues. "Man, I'm sorry." She blew her nose and eyed Zoe's jacket. "I'll pay to have that cleaned for you."

"It's washable. I don't buy anything that isn't." She giggled. "Let me help." She plucked a tissue from the packet and scrubbed at Mac's cheeks under her eyes. "That's better."

"I've never lost it that way." Mac glanced around. "I hope I didn't make too big a scene."

"Pfft." Zoe flipped her hand in the air. "If they get upset, that's their problem."

Mac stuffed the soggy tissues in her jacket pocket. "Let's go back to the office."

"Great." Zoe took her arm and headed for the car. "And on the way, we can talk."

Or not. How long a walk was it from here to the office? But she climbed into Zoe's little SUV and resigned herself to her fate.

"I think Mr. Underwood was really rattled, don't you?" Zoe signaled and pulled away from the curb.

Mac threw her a look of surprise. "We're talking about the case?"

"Well, yeah. What else?"

"Nothing. I just thought ..."

Zoe cast a quick look at her. "Hey, I know something is bothering you, and I figure when you're ready to talk about it, you will. I'll be here to listen. That's what friends are for. Right?"

"Right. Thanks, Zoe."

"So, what did you think of Underwood?"

"I agree with you. He was shook up ... but he knows more than he's telling us." Mac pursed her lips. "I should have pressed him like you said. Now, I may not get the chance."

"You'll get at it. I've seen you work. You're good."

"I guess the next thing is to confront Laura." Mac shook her head. "I just hate doing that in the hospital."

"I only have one question." Zoe stopped at a light and turned to Mac.

"What's that?"

"Can we get something to eat first? I'm starving."

AFTER A COUPLE OF HOURS, there was still no sign of Zane. Jake scanned the scene outside the SUV once more. "Maybe he's on foot?"

"But where would he go?" Vic asked.

"Does he have any other relatives in the area?"

Vic shook his head. "Not that we could find."

"Get a search warrant for his sister's house." Jake started the SUV. "We can't sit here any longer."

"Look." Vic stared out the window.

A white Toyota Camry raced past them. Jake slammed the SUV into gear and took off in a cloud of dust. At the intersection with Holtgrewe Road, the car swung right and accelerated. Jake followed with lights ablaze and siren blasting. Instead of slowing down, the car sped up.

"All units in the vicinity of Holtgrewe and One-Hundred. I'm in pursuit of a white Toyota Camry four-door. May contain murder suspect."

"You think he's headed for One-Hundred? He could turn right on Pottery." Vic yelled over the screaming siren.

"One-Hundred's his best bet of getting away."

The car made a left onto Pottery and headed for the stoplight at Highway One-Hundred.

"We got him now."

The light was red. Cars on the highway streamed past from both directions. But the Toyota showed no sign of stopping. Jake gripped the steering wheel. Fear of what he was about to witness soured his stomach.

"What's he doing?" Vic roared.

At the last possible second, the white car jerked right and rumbled along the shoulder. Horns blared at the speeding car until a van slowed to let him into the line of traffic. And just like that, the Camry was gone.

Jake pounded the steering wheel before grabbing his mic. "All units. The Camry is eastbound on Highway One-Hundred. I need units on Highway Forty-Seven and One-Hundred to intercept." He eased forward into traffic, sounding his siren in short blasts. "Can you see him?"

Vic lowered his window and stuck his head out. "No." He raised it again as he heard a call come in on the radio.

"We got him, Detective. He made a left on Forty-Seven headed for the bridge. We're going to box him in between Fifth and Sixth."

Jake signaled to change lanes and flipped another switch. "Police. Move over." The cars and trucks cleared a lane, and soon he was turning left onto Forty-Seven.

When he reached Sixth Street, police cars had the street blocked, and the white Toyota was halfway onto the sidewalk on the wrong side of the street. Jake and Vic jumped from the SUV and strode over to the Camry.

An officer met them. "He tried to make a run for it into the park, but we caught him." He inclined his head toward a police car. "He's over there."

Jake and Vic followed him to the squad car. The officer opened the back door, and Jake bent down.

He couldn't believe his eyes. "Get him out of there, please."

"Sure." The officer helped the man out onto the street.

"That's not Zane." Jake turned to Vic. "That's not our guy."

"Then who is he?"

"Good question." Jake narrowed his eyes at the man. "You heard him. Who are you?"

"I'm his brother-in-law."

Jake stepped closer. "Where's Zachary Zane?"

He shrugged. "I got no idea."

"You might want to rethink that answer." Icicles hung on Jake's words, but they had no effect on the man. He turned to the officer. "Book him for careless and imprudent driving, and with obstruction of justice." He tilted his head toward his SUV. "Let's go."

"I got the search warrant." Vic held up his phone to show Jake.

"Good." Jake yanked the SUV into reverse. "Might as well put out a BOLO for the truck again."

"I'll get officers to meet us at the house."

Jake knew what they'd find, and he was right. The old truck with the blue driver's door was gone. He hated being played. Twice. In one day. He ran a hand down his face. It was going to be hard to keep his calm. "Vic, you better take the lead on this one."

The officers suited up and grabbed the battering ram in case of resistance. Jake and Vic walked up the driveway.

"Wait." Jake detoured to the garage. He cupped his hands around his eyes and looked into the dark space. "The truck's in there."

"You're kidding." Vic came up next to him and peered in. "I don't get it. Why would the brother-in-law lead us around unless it was to give Zane time to escape?"

"Something stinks." Jake wrinkled his nose.

"Yeah."

"No, I mean for real. Something stinks. Can't you smell that?" Sudden understanding hit Jake. "Run."

"What?"

"Go. Gasoline. The place is about to—"

Jake dove for the ground, but a huge fist of energy slammed into his back and flung him across the drive. A mighty whump slapped his ears like two big hands, blowing out his eardrums. He curled into a ball and prayed he'd survive the pounding of the debris raining down from the sky.

# CHAPTER 14

The aroma of grilling hamburgers and fries at Wimpy's reminded Mac how hungry she was. "I'm glad you suggested this. We needed the break."

"And the protein. Good brain food." Zoe wiped ketchup from around her mouth and tossed her napkin on the table. "I love their burgers."

"Ready to get going again?" Mac pushed away from the table.

"Yup." Zoe stood and slipped into her jacket.

The familiar wail of sirens reached Mac's ears a block from the hospital. "Pull over." She strained to see the direction they were coming from. "Do you see them?"

"Not yet, but they're close. I'm staying put till they pass."

Three ambulances appeared from out of nowhere and raced past them toward the hospital. Mac's cellphone vibrated in her hand as the last one went by. It was Sam.

"Get to the hospital. Jake's been in an explosion. I'm on my way."

*Dear Lord, no.* Mac's hand tightened on her phone. She pressed End. "Hurry. Jake's in one of those ambulances."

"What happened?"

"An explosion." A terrible chill invaded her body, and all she could do was murmur, "Please Lord, no," over and over.

"I'll drop you at the emergency room door." Zoe punched the accelerator and maneuvered through the parking lot like a racecar driver. "Get out."

Mac had her belt undone before the car stopped. She jumped from the SUV and ran into the hospital. "My fiancé, Jake Sanders. Where is he?"

A nurse came out and stood in front of her. "Calm down. He's stable."

Mac closed her eyes and let the nurse's words sink in. "Where is he?"

"He's in surgery." The nurse held her hands up, palms out.

"Where should I go?" Hot tears filled Mac's eyes and dread sat like a stone in the pit of her stomach.

"There's a surgery waiting room on the second floor. They'll keep you informed."

Mac nodded and hurried for the elevators.

"Mac, where's my brother? Is he okay?" Sam walked as fast as she could to catch up, her hands supporting her baby belly. Miss P and Zoe kept pace on either side of her.

The sight of her friends broke Mac's reserve, and the tears that threatened a moment ago spilled down her face.

"What is it?" Sam stumbled and Zoe grabbed her.

The look of pain on Sam's face made her stomach clench. What was wrong? Her tears. "No, Sam." Mac swiped at her cheeks. "I was just crying because ... I guess I just lost it."

"You scared me." Sam leaned on Zoe. "I need to sit."

"I'm sorry." Mac pulled a chair over. "He's in surgery. According to the nurse, he's hurt, but stable."

"Next time, tell me he's okay before breaking down." Sam glared at her.

"I promise." Although she wasn't sure how many next times she could handle. "The nurse said there's a waiting room upstairs. Are you okay to head up there?"

"Yes." Sam levered herself out of the chair. "Thankfully, it's only a couple more months before this baby girl makes her appearance. It's getting harder and harder to move around."

"Sam." Alan jogged across the room and took her in his arms. "Baby. I heard what happened to Jake."

"He's okay. We're headed to the second-floor waiting room." She clung to her husband.

"Mackenzie, my dear, are you all right?" Miss P took her by the arm.

"I keep thinking about what you said the other night."

"I'm an old woman." Miss P squeezed her arm. "Do not let anything I say bother you."

"It's just that you said I might regret it if I waited to marry Jake." Mac blinked to clear her eyes, determined not to cry again. "When I heard Jake had been in an explosion, that's all I could think about."

"Mackenzie, I shouldn't have said that to you." Miss P stepped into the elevator.

When they exited on the second floor, Mac pulled her aside. "What do you mean, Miss P?"

"I waited to marry my husband." The older woman gave a slight wave of her hand. "I always had an excuse. He was traveling too much. I was teaching, and it was still frowned upon if a teacher married." She folded her hands in front of her. "When I finally agreed, we had a beautiful life together. But he got sick and passed away. All I could think about was how many years I wasted when I could have spent them with that wonderful man. I'm afraid I projected my hurt onto your situation. I shouldn't have done that."

Mac took her hands. "Miss P, I treasure everything you tell me because I know it comes from the heart." She gave the woman's hands a little shake. "And I'm independent enough to listen to you, but do what I think is best for me. So don't ever feel guilty about giving me advice."

"You remind me of myself." Miss P let go of Mac's hands and folded them in front of her once more. "Which isn't always a good thing, but you are precious to me. And so is Samantha. Now, shall we see if there's any news about Detective Sanders?"

The stone was back in Mac's stomach. She wasn't good at waiting. Especially when it was for news about someone she loved. The small waiting room contained a few more people than she'd expected.

"Mackenzie." Chief Baker removed his hat and swiped a hand across his bald head. "How you holding up?"

"I'm okay. What happened?"

He took her arm and guided her over to a corner. "Jake and Vic took some officers back to Zane's sister's house with a search warrant. When they got there, the truck was in the garage and Jake smelled gasoline a minute before it blew." The Chief rubbed his forehead. "If he hadn't, we'd have four dead policemen instead of one in surgery, one in ICU, and two with burns."

"I had no idea four guys were hurt. Who's in ICU?"

"Vic. He got hit with a piece off the truck and lost a lot of blood." The Chief heaved a sigh. "But he's going to be okay. They got the bleeding stopped and he's resting. I got to talk to him briefly before I came here."

Her legs went weak and she plopped into a nearby chair.

Jake and Vic, and two other officers. "Why?" She looked up at him.

He shrugged. "We think Zane switched the fuses in the box at the historic museum, but we're pretty sure he was working for somebody else. Maybe his boss decided to clean up loose ends."

"Was Zane in the house?" Horror lodged in her throat.

"We think so, and his sister."

Mac dropped her head into her hands, unable to speak. So much hurt and pain.

A doctor in scrubs entered the room and scanned the anxious faces turned his way. "Mrs. Majors?"

Sam raised her hand.

# CHAPTER 15

Mac and the rest of the people in the room closed in around Sam and the doctor.

"We finished setting your brother's broken shoulder." The doctor removed his cap and ruffled his damp hair. "He's lucky. Other than that, his injuries are minor. Bruising and scrapes. He'll be hurting. Some of the bruises are deep tissue, but no organ injuries or bones broken other than his shoulder."

A collective release of tension swept the room. Jake was going to be all right.

"Thank you, doctor." Sam struggled to stand, but the physician motioned her to stay in her chair.

"I've helped my wife go through two pregnancies." He gave her a warm smile. "Is this your first?"

"It is." Alan beamed at him. "A girl."

"I've got one of each. They're both gifts. Congratulations." He looked around. "Looks like you've got a good support group."

"We do, and so does Jake." Alan pulled Mac forward. "This is his fiancée, Mackenzie Love."

"Congratulations to you too." He gave her a little nod. "When's the happy occasion?"

"We haven't set the date yet." Mac gave him a shaky smile.

"Well, it shouldn't take too long for him to be ready to walk down the aisle." The doctor headed for the door. "If you'll excuse me."

"Doc, before you go, I'm his boss, Chief Baker." The Chief held out his hand to shake. "When can I get in to talk to Jake?"

"He's in recovery now. I'd give it another ... hour. Then check with the nurse at the desk in the hall." He nodded and offered a grim smile before closing the door behind him.

Mac scanned the room. Sam, Alan, Miss P, and Zoe were deep in conversation at the far end. She turned to the Chief. "I have a favor to ask. Make that two favors."

"What are they?" He narrowed his eyes at her.

"I came here originally to interview Laura James." She held his gaze. "I'm assuming you have an officer outside Doug's room. Will you call him and put me on the list of visitors so I can get in to speak to Laura?"

"What's the second favor?" The Chief's voice dropped to a gruff whisper.

"I want to see Jake, but I'm not family." The lump in her throat grew.

His stony gaze softened. "I'll make sure you get to visit Jake." He clamped his hat on his head. "As for the other, if you can give me a good reason, I'll consider it."

"Doug's aunt hired us to look into his electrocution. She doesn't think it's an accident."

"Why didn't she come to us?" He glowered at her.

"She told us she wanted evidence before going to the

police." Mac shrugged. "And, she's pretty sure Laura had something to do with it. I'm just doing my job, Chief."

He rubbed a hand down his face. "I'll make the call."

"Thank you." Mac gave his arm a brief touch. "What room is he in?"

"Three-ten." The stern voice was back. "Keep me informed of what you learn."

"I will." Mac slipped out the door into the hall. One floor up. She headed for the stairs.

An officer sat outside a door about halfway down the third-floor hallway. She took a deep breath and walked toward the man as if she belonged there. Hopefully, the Chief had made the call.

"Hello. I'm Private Investigator Mackenzie Love. Chief Baker called and put me on the visitor list?" She gave him a confident smile. Never let them see you sweat. That's what her daddy had always said.

"Just got off the phone with him." The officer ticked her name off. "Go on in."

The entrance to the room was set back about three feet. As Mac approached, the raised voices of two women reached her through the closed door. She paused to listen.

"No." A vaguely familiar voice wailed. "You can't do that. I just found out you were getting a divorce anyway."

"Yes, I can, and what business is it of yours whether I was getting a divorce or not?" The cool voice of Laura James. "I'm still his wife and power of attorney."

"But he may come out of the coma. He may come back to me—us."

"You heard the doctor. There's no sign of brain activity. You're a nurse. You know what that means."

That's where she'd heard the voice. The woman was

Francis Underwood, the nurse who'd administered CPR to Doug.

"Doctors get it wrong all the time." The pain in Francis's voice was palpable. "If you shut down all the machines now, it will be murder."

"That's a little dramatic, Francis. Especially since the electrocution was an accident in the first place."

"How—"

"Be quiet." Laura James hissed. "You have nothing to say about it. Doug would not want to be a vegetable the rest of his life. And I don't want to have to deal with an invalid."

"You don't love him. You never did."

The sound of a chair scraping across the tile floor reached Mac a moment before the door slammed open. Francis Underwood barreled past Mac, tears streaming down her face.

Laura looked up as Mac stepped into the room. "What do you want?"

"I came to see how you're holding up." She righted the chair on the other side of the bed and sat. The whir of machines provided a constant background noise in the dimly lit room.

"Why? We hardly know each other." She plopped into a chair.

"I know what it feels like to sit next to the hospital bed of the man I love." Mac glanced at the still form of Douglas James lying between them. If she hadn't known it was him, she wouldn't have recognized his blanketed form with all the tubes and bandages.

"You mean Jake. He's quite a guy."

"Thanks." A flash of jealousy took her by surprise, and she lowered her gaze to her hands to hide it from the other woman. "Doug is too."

"Yeah." Laura squirmed in her chair. "He was. Is. The

doctors say there's no activity in his brain. But once, I saw his eyelids flutter, and every so often, his fingers move. The doctors tell me that's normal, but I don't know what to do."

"That's tough." Mac looked at her. The conversation she'd overheard made it sound like Laura had made up her mind.

"The *friend* of his who was just here thinks I should give it more time." She spat the word as if it tasted bitter. "She thinks he might come out of it. What do you think?"

Mac studied the woman across from her. What should she say? "I'm afraid I can't help you. What does your heart say?"

"My heart was leading me to a divorce before this happened." Laura stared at Doug. "Now …"

"Was Doug okay with a divorce?" Wait. Didn't Doug's aunt say he wanted the divorce, and Laura was fighting it? Could Mac be getting close to a motive?

"No." Laura's face darkened as her gaze hardened into a glare at the man on the bed between them. "He kept saying we'd work it out. But I was through trying to 'work it out.'" She air-quoted the last phrase. "Now I guess I have no choice."

"You have a choice." Mac lowered her voice. "You can choose whether Doug continues like this or not. Not a decision I would want to make."

Laura snapped her head up to look at Mac.

Mac held her gaze. So far, it was attempted murder, but if she decided to turn off the machines and Doug didn't survive, that would change. Was Laura the one who convinced Zane to switch the fuses? Better a widow than divorced?

Was Laura a black widow like Zoe suggested?

# CHAPTER 16

Mac debated on whether to push Laura any further. She'd stopped too soon with Thomas Underwood and regretted it. But this situation was different. Doug lay in the bed in a coma. How much had he heard of their conversation? If he really didn't have any brain activity, probably nothing.

"What are you thinking?" Laura asked.

"I'm wondering just how badly you wanted out of your marriage." There, she'd said it. Mac's pulse ramped up.

Laura's mouth dropped open for a moment before her face grew purple with rage. "Get out." She jumped to her feet and flung her arm toward the door. "I don't ever want to see you again."

A calm detachment filled Mac as she got to her feet and walked from the room. Laura hadn't questioned what Mac meant by her statement. Laura already knew someone had tried to kill Doug. Did she do it?

Or was she left to finish what someone else started—someone like Thomas Underwood?

Mac pushed through the door into the hall. A hand grabbed her arm.

"Would you please tell this officer that it's okay for me to go in to see Doug?"

Her gaze traveled from the hand on her arm up to the face of Thomas Underwood, and she tensed. He must have seen the look in her eye because he released her. "You have to clear it through Chief Baker, the Chief of Police."

"That's ridiculous." He threw his hands in the air. "I'm Doug's partner."

"What's going on?" Laura stepped out with a scowl on her face. "I thought I heard your voice. What's the problem, Thom?"

"This officer won't let me into the room." Underwood made a sweeping gesture toward the man in uniform.

"Oh, crying out loud. Come on." She grabbed his sleeve and dragged him toward the door to Doug's room.

"But, ma'am." The officer trailed after them. "He's not on the list."

Mac chuckled under her breath. "Good luck, officer." She turned and headed for the nurse's station.

"Can I help you?"

"I need the room number for Jake Sanders."

"He's in the ICU."

"I know. I'm his fiancée." Mac glanced at her bare ring finger. With no way to prove it. "Chief Baker was going to clear it with them for me to visit Jake."

"ICU is through those doors." The nurse inclined her head to the left. "At the end of the hall."

"Thanks." Again, Mac prayed the Chief could clear the way for her once more. At the double doors, she pressed the button and explained who she was through the intercom. The doors opened. *Thank You, Jesus. And Chief Baker.*

Another nurses' station with another nurse. "I'm Mackenzie Love, Jake Sander's fiancée."

"Love. Love." The nurse ran her finger down the computer screen. "Here it is. Detective Sanders is in room three. Over there." She pointed to her left.

Mac's anxiety grew with every step she took toward Jake's open door. When she arrived, her first glimpse of him almost buckled her knees. Except for the bruising under his eyes, he was almost as white as the bandages swathing his left shoulder and arm. Tubes and wires tethered him to machines that beeped and whirred.

Just like Doug.

Chief Baker stepped between her and Jake. "It's not as bad as it looks." He took her arm and steered her to two chairs in the hall. "Sit."

She did as she was told and turned to the Chief, begging him with her eyes to answer the question she couldn't put into words.

"He's fine. He's resting." The Chief took off his hat and placed it on his lap. "When he wakes up, you'll see. He's good."

She drew in a shaky breath and released it on a prayer. "I just came from Doug James."

"Oh." He scratched his chin. "I could see how it would be easy to think Jake was …" He shrugged. "But take my word for it, not even close."

"Do they allow drinks back here? I could use a soft drink."

"I'll get us a couple." The Chief donned his hat and left.

Mac rose and tiptoed into Jake's room. The pain in her chest tightened like a vise around her heart. She wanted her big, strong, pig-headed man back. She bent close to his ear and whispered. "I love you, Jake Sanders."

"There you are." The Chief stood at the open door and held up two soft drinks.

She ran her eyes over the familiar angles of Jake's face one more time before joining Chief Baker in the hall. He handed her a can wrapped in a napkin.

"Thanks."

"You feel better now?"

"Yeah." She nodded and took a sip.

"What did Laura James have to say?" He gave her a sideways look.

Her talk with Laura seemed like days ago. What did she say? Mac furrowed her brow in concentration. "The argument." Her brow relaxed.

"What argument?"

"When I got to the room, I overheard an argument between her and Francis Underwood. Laura wants to unplug the machines from Doug and let him go. Francis wants her to wait."

"What business is it of this Francis Underwood's?"

"It's just an impression." Mac took another sip. "But, I helped her do CPR on Doug before the EMTs arrived, and I think she's in love with him."

"Who is she?"

"Her brother, Thomas Underwood, is Doug's partner. I understand that Francis is a friend of the family. She's also a nurse."

"I better get this down." The Chief searched his coat pockets for his notebook. "So who won?"

"I'm not sure. Francis left in a huff." A nurse entered Jake's room to take his vitals, and Mac lost her train of thought.

"Mac." The Chief nudged her.

"Sorry." She blinked. "Francis left and I went in." Mac went on to tell the Chief what Laura said about being unsure what to do, saying it was she who wanted a divorce, and then the whole scene with Underwood. She also informed him of what Miss P found out about Laura and Thomas Underwood.

The Chief shook his head. "I was trying to keep my suspects away from each other as much as possible."

"Sorry."

"Not your fault." But his gruff voice indicated how upset he was.

"How about you? What have you guys discovered about Zane?"

His eyes widened. "You don't know?"

"Know what?"

"Jake got caught in the bomb when he and Vic went back to Zane's sister's house to serve a search warrant. We think Zane was working for someone else and that someone decided to clean up loose ends." The Chief rubbed his forehead. "Zane and his sister were probably both in the house when it blew up."

Someone like Laura or Underwood? Or both? "When was this?" Adrenaline and caffeine sparked her heart rate.

"A little before three."

"Laura wasn't at home when we went by at one-thirty. We assumed she was at the hospital." Mac searched her memory. "And Zoe and I were at lunch. We'd left Thomas Underwood about forty-five minutes before that."

"It's easy to check if Laura was here." The Chief dug for his cellphone in his jacket pocket. "Underwood might be harder."

His phone vibrated in his hand before he could punch a number. "Chief Baker." Confusion clouded his expression, followed by frustration. "Are you sure?" He raised his hands palms out. "Yeah. I get it. Okay. Put out an APB on Zachary Zane." He punched End.

"What was that all about?"

"It seems only one person got caught in the bomb." Chief Baker shook his head. "Zane's sister."

# CHAPTER 17

"Could Zane have set the bomb?" Mac found it hard to believe a person could do such a thing, knowing his sister would be killed in the blast.

"We'll know more later." The Chief got up. "I need to move. I'm going to talk to the officer outside Doug James's room and see when Laura James got here."

Mac nodded. Sam's familiar voice sounded to her left at the nurse's station. Mac jumped to her feet. "Over here."

Sam turned. She looked tired, and her beautiful blonde hair had lost its luster. Tears pricked the backs of Mac's eyes while guilt pinched her heart. She'd been so wrapped up in her own sorrow that she hadn't thought about how hard this must be for Sam. "Hello, my friend." Mac crossed to her and offered her arm for support.

Sam gave her a brief smile and took her arm. "How is he?"

"He's resting." Mac prepared to catch her friend when she first saw her brother. "Sam, Chief Baker assures me Jake's fine, but he's looking pretty rough."

But when they got to the open door, Jake smiled at them,

his blue eyes gleaming in the artificial gloom. "There are my two favorite gals," he said, his voice ragged.

Mac let out the breath she hadn't realized she'd been holding in. "The Chief was right. You are fine." She let go of Sam and rushed to Jake's side.

"Not yet. Getting there." He swallowed and grimaced. "Throat hurts."

"That's from the air tube during surgery." Sam eased into a chair next to his bed. "You've got to stop this nonsense. At least while I'm carrying your niece." She patted her baby bulge. "It's not good for me to get these scares so close to the end."

He gave a thumbs-up.

"There you guys are." Alan swept into the room and kissed the top of Sam's head.

Mac looked for somewhere she could touch Jake, but every inch was covered in bandages, bruises, or tubes. Except one small patch of skin on his right forearm.

When she placed a finger on his arm, Jake gave her the look that always made her stomach flip. A smile filled with love and hope for the future lifted the sides of her mouth.

"Excuse me." A petite nurse glided into the room. "I need to take care of my patient." She tilted her head at them and held up two slim fingers of a gloved hand. "Only two of you at a time. One must go."

"I'll go." Mac moved around Sam and Alan. "I've been here the longest. You need time with your brother." She gazed at Jake. "I'll be back tomorrow." As she exited the ICU, Zoe rushed over.

"How are you doing?" She hugged Mac. "How's Jake?"

Mac gave her a squeeze and backed away. It was easier to answer the question about Jake. "He's awake and in good spirits. Hurting from his injuries but seems okay." As for herself ...

"Great." Zoe took her arm. "Miss P had to leave. Something about her nephew."

"Nate."

"Yeah. Nate." In the waiting room, Zoe faced Mac. "What now? Are you ready to go home?"

Mac nodded.

"Great. Let's go."

"My car's at the office. You can drop me there."

"Or I can take you home and pick you up tomorrow?" Zoe raised her eyebrows at Mac.

That sounded good, but she hated being without a car. The doors *whooshed* open into the night. A chill March wind penetrated Mac's blouse. "Thanks, but I think I'd rather you take me to the office."

Zoe jabbered about the doctors and nurses as she drove them across town. Mac closed her eyes and tried not to think about what was happening to the people she loved. And to her.

Sam was a little over seven months pregnant and had her own problems to deal with. Alan needed to take care of Sam. Jake was laid up in the hospital with a broken shoulder. Miss P was dealing with an ex-con nephew and helping with Sam. And Mac's sisters lived in Kansas City. The last time she felt like the ground beneath her feet had given way was when her parents died. She knew she was being dramatic and needed to snap out of it, but she wasn't sure how.

They pulled into the driveway at the office. Light spilled onto the porch.

"I need to go in and button things up before heading home." Mac opened the car door. "Thanks for today."

"No problem. I like being part of the group." She nodded toward the house that served as the offices for the private investigators. "Do you need some help?"

"No. It's only a matter of turning off lights and setting the alarm." Mac shut the car door and waved. She waited for Zoe to back out before taking the steps to the covered porch.

The surrounding bushes and trees combined with the roof left corners of the porch in deep shadow, and Mac fumbled with her key. She finally pressed the flashlight app on her phone to light the lock.

A split second before she was about to open the door, a whiff of smoke mixed with body odor and an aroma she associated with fear froze her in place. A man knocked her to the side and pressed her against the wall.

"I did not know." Zane pushed his face within inches of hers. "I did what I was told."

"Know what?" Mac pulled her hands into tight fists. Adrenaline surged through her.

"What would happen with the fuses," he hissed at her between clenched teeth.

"Then you need to talk to the police." She concentrated on keeping her voice calm and her face from reacting to his stale breath. "Tell them who's behind this."

"They are friends with—"

"Let her go." Nate bounded up the steps and lunged at Zane.

Zane swung around and punched Nate in the stomach. The ex-lawyer doubled over. Zane cocked his arm, ready to deliver another blow.

"Stop." Mac grabbed him.

He shook her off, vaulted off the porch, and ran into the darkness.

# CHAPTER 18

Mac stared after Zane, filled with frustration. She whirled around. "He was about to tell me who hired him. I can't believe you did that."

"Rescue you, you mean?" He braced himself with one hand against the wall of the house. The other arm hugged his middle. "Sorry." Sarcasm dripped from every word.

"Okay. Yeah." She pinched the bridge of her nose. "Thanks. You might as well come in."

"I have to pay for my cab first." He swung an arm to where a taxi sat at the curb.

The familiar sound of sirens split the night air.

"Uh-oh." He cringed. "I think the cabbie called the police."

Mac covered her face with her hands as two patrol cars pulled up.

"I'll take care of this." Nate hobbled across the lawn to the cab.

She sat on the porch swing and waited as Nate and the cabbie talked to the police. One patrol car and the cab left. Nate and an officer trudged up the slight incline back to the porch.

"Let's go inside and sit down." Mac rose and opened the door.

"Thanks, Ms. Love." The officer inclined his head. "I'll get your statement and be on my way."

She led them to the couch and chairs in the reception area and dropped into one of the chairs. Nate eased onto the sofa, and the officer perched on the other chair.

After relating how Zane accosted her and their conversation, she turned to Nate and tried to keep her tone of voice even. "I imagine Nate has told you how he came to my rescue."

"Yes, ma'am." The officer closed his notebook and stood. "I'll be going. We'll keep an eye on the office and your home tonight."

"Thanks. I'd appreciate that." Mac walked the officer to the door.

"And when you see Detective Sanders, tell him we're all rooting for him to get better soon."

"I'll tell him." She closed the door and turned to see Nate staring at her.

"My aunt told me Jake was in the hospital. That's why she sent me to see if you're all right." He ran a hand through his hair. "She tried to reach Zoe but couldn't."

"I see." Mac headed for the kitchen. So, Nate was the last resort. "I need a glass of iced tea. You want anything?"

"The same." Nate strolled around the room. "What happened to Jake?"

"He was in a bomb blast. He has a broken shoulder."

"Ouch."

"Yeah." She handed him a glass and went back to her chair. "Why didn't Miss P come herself? Although I'm glad she didn't."

"She was going back to the hospital to be with Sam. I guess

she's pretty anxious, and Miss P was making her some special hot tea?"

Mac chuckled. "That sounds like her."

"I wouldn't put it past her to show up at your house tonight." Nate gulped iced tea and held it up to the light.

"Me either."

"Couldn't get decent tea in prison. Couldn't get much of anything decent, to be honest." He placed his glass on the side table with care and planted his feet on the floor in front of him. Leaning forward, he dropped his head to his chest. When he raised it, his eyes caught hers in a look of openness and sincere honesty. "I meant what I said the other day in your driveway, Mac."

"I know. And I appreciate it." She let her eyes roam over the lines of the face that was once so familiar to her.

His hair had grown out, and it wasn't hard to remember the long locks Nate wore in college—almost as long as hers. The shadow of a beard and mustache completed the picture. An older but wiser version of the face she knew back then. But what they had back then wasn't love.

He scooted his chair closer.

She knew real love. Jake's rugged face, with its nose broken at least once and a smile that revealed slightly crooked teeth, filled her mind. Warmth spread across her chest. The image changed to one of Jake in the hospital bed.

Nate reached for her hand. "Are you thinking about the day we went to the beach?"

"What?" She tensed. "No. I was thinking about Jake. I need to go home." She jumped to her feet. "Thanks for coming to check on me and rescuing me."

"You're welcome." He sighed. "I'll help you close up."

"That's not necessary." She crossed to the door and pulled it open.

"I was hoping you'd give me a ride back to my aunt's." He raised his eyebrows and gave her a goofy grin.

"Oh." She clenched her fists. "Of course. Not a problem." But if he made a pass at her in the car …

"There you are." Miss P stepped through the open door. "I was worried about you two." Her gaze flitted between Mac and Nate.

"It's good to see you." Mac hugged her. "I had a run-in with Zane, and Nate appeared at just the right time. The police came, and I was about to close up the office and take Nate back to your place before going home."

"Excellent." Miss P turned off the lights in the reception area. "I will give Nathaniel a ride to my home before meeting you at yours."

"You don't have to do that."

"My dear." The elderly lady peered at her over her glasses. "Detective Sanders would never forgive me if I allowed anything to happen to you, and I would never forgive myself as well. I intend to spend the night with you as I have done before."

"You might as well go along with her." Nate winked at Mac over his aunt's shoulder. "She's an unstoppable force."

Mac placed a hand on the older woman's arm. "And I love her for it."

"Before I go," Nate rubbed the bridge of his nose, "I could help research your parents' accident. Aunt P told me you're looking into it."

"No." Mac held up a hand but stopped herself. Maybe she could use his help. "On second thought, there are some lawsuits involved, and I can't understand all the legalese. As you said, you may not be licensed to practice law, but you still know how. We'll talk tomorrow."

"Great. I'd like to help, and it would give me something to fill my time."

Mac secured the office and followed Miss P and Nate down the porch. Once inside her car, she dialed Sam's number.

"Hi, Mac."

"Oh no. Did I wake you?" She glanced at the time. Nine o'clock.

"Just resting my eyes. I'm about to go back in and see Jake. Where are you?"

"I'm leaving the office. I needed to retrieve my car and close it up before heading home." No way was she telling Sam about the visit from Zane. Or Nate. At least not now. "Sorry. Miss P and I left in a hurry."

"How's Jake?" Her plan was to go back to the hospital tomorrow morning, but Sam's answer could change that.

"He's good. The doctor seems to think he could be moved out of the ICU tomorrow."

Tension flowed from Mac's body, and with that came the tears.

"Mac? Are you there? Did you hear me?"

"Yes." Mac choked out the word around the lump in her throat. "Good news."

"Oh, honey. Now you've got me crying."

"Yeah, but you're pregnant. You can blame it on hormones."

"We're women." Sam chuckled. "Since when do we need an excuse to cry?"

"But we're professional investigators."

"Well, I won't tell anyone if you don't."

Mac barked a laugh. "You're the best friend a woman could ever want."

"Ditto. Now get some sleep. Because I intend to."

"I promise not to call unless it's an emergency." Mac swiped the tears from her face.

She'd slowed while on the phone, and a dark sedan swerved around her and sped off. Time to focus on getting home. But at the corner of High and Sixth Streets, she found a car blocking the road, and a woman stood outside waving her arms. It was the sedan that had passed her in such a hurry.

# CHAPTER 19

Mac let her car glide to a stop fifty feet from the vehicle blocking her way and peered at the woman who was shielding her eyes from Mac's headlights. It was Francis Underwood. Mac opened her door and climbed out. "Miss Underwood, are you having car trouble?"

"No, Miss Love." She scurried over. "I know this seems odd, but I need to talk to you alone, and every time I tried, you had people around."

All sorts of alarms started sounding in Mac's brain. "Why don't we go to my house? We can talk there." And Miss P would be there shortly. Not to mention, Mac's gun.

"No." Francis rubbed her hands together as if washing them. "I prefer to talk here."

Mac scanned the road. No lights appeared in the few houses nearby. "Let me get my phone. Sam is supposed to call me and if I don't answer, she's likely to call the police." Mac shrugged. "She's pregnant. Hormones. You understand."

"Sadly, I don't." Francis shuffled her feet. "I thought at one time ..."

"What is it you want to talk to me about, Francis?"

The woman took a step closer. Her breath came so quickly Mac was afraid she'd pass out. Actually, maybe that wouldn't be such a bad thing.

"She's going to kill him." Francis's voice broke.

Ah, the argument at the hospital. But Mac wasn't supposed to know anything about that. "Who?"

"Laura, Doug's wife." Francis collapsed against the hood of Mac's car. "We need to stop her."

"How is she going to kill him?" Mac took a small step away from the woman and glanced at her phone. Could she dial nine-one-one without Francis noticing? But was this an emergency—was the woman a danger to her, or just distraught?

"She's going to stop all his support machines." The poor woman was wailing.

"Francis, please calm down. How can I help if you're so upset?" Mac spoke in a low, soothing voice. "We have to think logically. Make a plan."

She drew in several deep breaths and wiped her cheeks with the hems of her sleeves. "Yes. A plan. You're right."

"Do you know when Laura will be pulling ... stopping all the life-support systems?"

"No, but ... Maybe tomorrow." Her eyes filled with tears again.

"Can she do that so soon?"

"She told me she can do anything she wants because she's Doug's power of attorney."

"I have a lawyer friend who can help you with that aspect of it. Let me call him when I get home. He can research it, and I'll get back to you." Mac shivered. The temperature had dropped, and the wind picked up. "Why would Laura want her husband dead? Last I heard, she was already divorcing him."

"She never loved Doug." Francis spat. "Not like ..." She glanced at Mac.

*Not like she did?* Mac waited.

"She gets more with him dead than in a divorce. Life insurance and part-ownership of the company."

"But will the company continue without Doug?"

Francis blinked. "I don't know."

A car's headlights appeared a few blocks away.

"You're going to have to move your car." Mac opened the door to her car. "And I need to get home. We'll talk more tomorrow."

"Promise?"

"I promise." The naked need on the woman's face made Mac's heart ache. Didn't she have any friends to talk to? And what about her brother, Thomas? Francis turned and lumbered back to her car.

Could her brother have been involved in what happened to Doug? It was clear Thomas Underwood had a thing for Laura. Mac blinked away tears. Francis and Mac had worked so hard to save Doug's life. *Please, Lord, don't let Douglas James die.*

The headlights stopped behind Mac and waited for Francis and Mac to move, then followed Mac back to her house. Not again. Who was accosting her this time? Mac pulled her phone from her purse and pushed nine-one-one, but before she could complete the call, Miss P's late-model sedan pulled into the driveway behind her.

Miss P exited her car and strode toward Mac with slow, deliberate steps. "It seems I can't leave you on your own for more than ten minutes these days, young lady."

"That wasn't my doing." Mac tapped the middle of her chest. "Francis appeared out of nowhere and blocked the road."

"You didn't think to call nine-one-one?"

"You mean like I was about to do because someone was following me? Yes, but she wasn't threatening me. She wanted my help."

"Please retrieve my overnight bag from the sedan, and we can continue this conversation inside." Miss P folded her hands in front of her.

Mac yanked Miss P's suitcase from the backseat and grumbled her way up the walkway to her door. Her former chemistry teacher had a way of making her feel like she was back in high school instead of a grown woman with a fiancé and a thriving business.

"Thank you, Mackenzie." The older woman took her bag from Mac and set it next to the couch. "I'm sorry, my dear." She placed a hand on Mac's arm. "I shouldn't have spoken to you like I did. Please tell me what Francis had to say that was so urgent she had to ambush you on your way home."

"It's okay. I know everything you do is because you care about me." Mac dropped her purse on a chair and headed for the kitchen. "I'm starved. Would you like something?"

"Yes. Let me help you."

"Grilled cheese and tomato soup?"

"Excellent."

"If you'll get it started, I need to call Nate." Mac hurried back to her purse. "I've got another research project for him." He picked up after one ring.

"It's not tomorrow yet, is it?" He gave a throaty chuckle.

"No, but I have something else I want you to look into." Mac pulled two bowls off the cupboard shelf and handed them to Miss P. "I need to know if there's a time limit on shutting off the life support system of a coma patient."

Miss P raised her eyebrows at her.

"I already know the answer. I won't go into any details, but I had to look into it for my former bosses. If you get my drift."

The Chicago mafia. Mac leaned against the kitchen counter.

"There's no federal or state law about when a life support system can be shut down, but as with most things, there's a general consensus—to wait at least seventy-two hours."

"Seventy-two hours," Mac repeated the information.

"Why do you want to know?"

"For a case." She looked at a calendar hanging on the wall. Tomorrow morning would be seventy-two hours since Doug's electrocution.

# CHAPTER 20

Mac rubbed a fist against her aching chest. The glimmer of hope for Doug's recovery grew dimmer. "One more question. If the person is the victim in an ongoing investigation, can a lawyer stop anyone from turning off life support until the case is solved?"

"That depends. It's the doctors' call. If they feel continuing life support is not a benefit to the patient—that it's futile— they can legally and ethically stop it. No matter the circumstances."

"So, the family can't decide to have it turned off on their own?" The horizon brightened a little.

"Again, it's tricky. The family should be consulted in any case, and the patient may have a directive or a living will that must be honored." Silence. "This wouldn't be the electrician I read about in the newspaper, would it?"

"I'm not allowed to talk about it, but thanks for your help."

"Okay. I'll talk to you tomorrow about your parents' case. Sweet dreams, Mac."

"Goodnight." Questions swirled around in her brain like

leaves in an autumn wind. Did Doug have a living will? Who could request another brain activity test? What was Zane about to tell her before Nate arrived? All questions she didn't have answers to. She pushed away from the counter and strode to the table.

"Sit and eat." Miss P placed a gentle hand on her arm. "You need food."

At the sound of her voice, the delicious aromas of melted cheese and warm tomato soup broke through Mac's thoughts, and her stomach growled. "You are amazing, Miss P."

They said a short prayer before devouring the meal. By silent agreement, the women waited until the kitchen was clean before bringing up the business of the day.

"I take it that was Nate on the phone." Miss P folded a dish towel and hung it on the rack.

"Yes. I've asked him to help research my mom and dad's murder." Mac placed the two bowls back into the cupboard. "I'll speak to him tomorrow and give him the lawyer's files that Mrs. White gave me." She yawned. "I can't understand them anyway."

"An excellent idea." Miss P took her arm and led her out to the living room. "He seemed to be of help tonight as well."

Mac nodded. "But our talk left me with lots more questions."

"We should speak with Douglas's aunt again. I'll arrange a meeting in the morning."

"I'm going to the hospital first thing to see Jake, but after that, I'll be flexible."

Miss P rose. "Would you care for a hot tea before bed? Something to soothe you?"

"That would be nice." Mac smiled at her. She closed her eyes and concentrated on taking deep breaths. In and out. In and out. Had Sam been in touch with Doug's aunt? Had she visited him in the hospital? Did she know if he had a living will?

Her eyes popped open. Why hadn't they heard from her? Another nagging question that must wait until tomorrow for an answer.

AFTER SPENDING some time praying and drinking her tea, Mac finally slept. And, as usual, her best sleep was right before the alarm went off. She stretched and debated setting it for another fifteen minutes, but knew that would only make it harder to get up.

A soft knock sounded at the door. "Are you awake, Mackenzie? I am starting breakfast."

"Yes." That settled that. Mac swung her legs out of bed and headed for the shower.

Cleaned and dressed, she sat down to a breakfast of eggs, bacon, and toast. Oh man, she could get used to this. "Have I told you lately that you're amazing?"

Miss P chuckled. "Yes, dear."

"You're going to the office this morning?" Mac took her plate to the sink.

"Yes. I will gather the files for Nathaniel and call Ursula Green."

"I'm going to see Jake and … not sure what after that. I have a lot of questions I want answered."

"What about Zoe?"

Ah, Zoe. "She can take the files to Nate, for one thing." Mac chewed her lower lip. She hadn't figured out where Zoe fit into the group yet.

"Do you think that's wise?" Miss P peered at her over the

rim of her glasses. "They can both be, well, somewhat exuberant."

"I think we can trust her to deliver some documents." She hoped.

The two women exited the house through the garage. As the door whirred open, a chill wind raced in and stirred the dead leaves at their feet.

"Looks like it could snow." Mac pulled her coat tighter and studied the low-hanging clouds.

"We do get some of our biggest snowstorms in March." Miss P adjusted her gloves. "Be careful driving, Mackenzie."

"You too. Although that tank you drive can probably muscle its way through just about anything."

"This automobile has served me well for many years, I'll have you know. It is a classic." Miss P straightened. "Just like its owner."

"I don't know about the car, but I agree about you." Mac waved at Miss P. "See you later."

As Mac pulled into a space at the hospital, a few soft white flakes drifted down from the sky. "Here it comes." Washington had already had its share of snow for the year, and she prayed this was only a sprinkle as opposed to a storm.

When she texted Sam to see if she was at the hospital, she found out that Jake had been moved. Good news. Her steps lightened the closer she got to his room, and she pushed through the door with a huge smile on her face. She couldn't wait to see him.

Laura James leaned over Jake, pinning his good arm beneath her, with her arm on the pillow encircling his head, and she was kissing him. On the mouth. Ice-cold rage enshrouded Mac.

"Sorry to interrupt." Her voice cut the air like a scalpel. She threw her purse and coat on a chair.

"Oh." Laura jumped back with a sly grin. "I guess she caught us, Jake."

"There's no 'us,' Mrs. James." Jake's tone left no doubt about what happened.

The woman took advantage of his lack of mobility and weakened condition. The fact that it was Mac who walked in was just a bonus for her.

The rage inside Mac shifted into sympathy. *What makes a person so bitter and hateful?*

Laura must have seen the change in Mac's demeanor. Her eyes hardened. "Aren't you going to tell me to get out?"

"No," Mac said softly.

"But I am," Jake growled. He motioned for Mac to come closer.

"Wait." Mac held up her hands. "Before you go, how's Doug?"

"If you're asking if he's still on life support, yes. But I'm going there now. I intend to stop it." She gave them a cruel smile.

"Please, wait a little longer." Mac took a step closer with her arms outstretched.

"Why, Miss Love, anyone would think you were in love with my husband. Like that crazy nurse friend of his." She cast an ugly look at Jake. "What do you think about that, Detective Sanders?"

"Doug is her friend." Jake shot her a stony look in return. "Mac cares about her friends."

"He's *my* husband." Laura walked to the door and turned. "I'll do what I feel is best for him."

"Does Doug have a living will?" The question foremost on her mind came out in a rush.

"What business is it of yours?"

"None." Mac brought her voice down again. "Humor me."

"I don't know. I haven't seen one." She took a step into the room. "Does that make a difference?"

"It could." Mac approached her. "According to a lawyer friend of mine, stopping life support is basically up to the doctor. In consultation with the family, and making sure any living will or directive is honored."

"I guess I'd better convince the doctor then." She pivoted on her heel and left the room.

# CHAPTER 21

"I don't think she cares about living wills or Doug." Mac turned to face Jake. He had his eyes closed, his face rigid with ... anger? Or pain? "Are you okay?" She reached for his hand. He had them balled into fists. "What's wrong, Jake? Should I call a nurse?"

He skewered her with his eyes. "Who's the lawyer friend you told Laura about?"

"Nate." She held his gaze. "Jake, I know you love me, but do you trust me?"

"It's him I don't trust."

"What do you think is going to happen?" She glared at him. "Do you think he's going to hypnotize me? Get me to do something against my will?" She threw her arms up. "If that's the case, you don't know me as well as I thought you did."

"No. That's not what I think." He glared back. "I don't like the guy. Okay?"

"Well, too bad." She put her hands on her hips. "He has knowledge that's helpful to me right now, and I'm going to use him. He's working on my parents' case, and you're just going to have to be okay with that."

"I guess I'm worried." He cut his eyes away from her.

"About what?" She stepped closer.

He shrugged. "You two were an item once."

Mac put her arm on the pillow above his head and leaned over him. "Is this how it's done?" She brushed her lips against his.

"Very funny." He pulled her head down and pressed his lips to hers.

The alarm on his IV sounded.

"You are the only one I've ever loved." Mac stood as the nurse entered the room. "And ever will."

"Excuse me." The white-haired woman in blue scrubs yanked two gloves from the container on the wall. "I need to check Mr. Sanders's IV."

"Yes, ma'am." Mac stepped back and made a silly face at Jake over the nurse's bent form.

He bit his lip and turned his head.

"It seems fine." The nurse straightened. "Try not to crimp the line by moving your arm."

"Do you know how much longer they plan on keeping me here?" Jake gave the nurse his best puppy dog look.

"I'll see if I can find out for you." She patted his good shoulder, pulled off her gloves, and left.

"Jake Sanders, you've been in a bomb blast. Do not leave this hospital until the doctor thinks you're ready." Mac steeled her gaze.

"I won't." He raised his right hand off the bed. "I promise. Now, where were we?"

"Oh no." Mac wagged a finger at him. "I've got work to do, and I refuse to be responsible for any more alarms going off."

"What are you doing?" His tone sharpened.

"Miss P is arranging another meeting with Doug's aunt for one thing." She pulled on her coat. "And I'm going to call my older sister, Beth, to see what she remembers about Francis Underwood."

"Why Francis Underwood? Isn't she the nurse who helped you do CPR on Doug?"

Mac nodded.

"Something bothered you that day. I could tell, but never got a chance to ask you. What was it?"

"It was just a feeling—a feeling that I found out is true." Mac pulled her gloves on. "Francis Underwood is in love with Doug James."

"The crazy nurse friend that Laura mentioned." Jake nodded.

"The same." Mac walked over to the side of his bed. "She asked me to help stop Laura from shutting off Doug's life support. At least for a few more days. That's why I called Nate. To see if there were any legal ways of doing it. There aren't." Mac sighed. "Another call I have to make, and one I'm not looking forward to. I have to tell Francis what I found out."

Jake slid his hand across the bed toward her. "I'm sorry."

Mac removed her glove and took his hand. "Me too."

"I hate—"

"I know." She caressed his face. "You concentrate on getting better so you can get out of here. I miss you so much."

He nodded. "Be careful out there."

"Always."

Mac retraced her steps through the hospital outside and paused under the overhang. The wind swirled the powdery snow in the parking lot into mini whirling dervishes like white dust devils. She flipped her hood up and hurried to her car.

"So much for sprinkles." Snow covered the roof and trailed down the windshield to the hood. She slid behind the steering wheel, slammed the door, and started the engine. "Snowstorms in March. Haven't we had enough of this stuff?" She glared through the windshield at the curtain of white flakes pouring down from the sky. The Pink Panther theme sounded from her car speakers. She pressed a button on her steering wheel. "Mackenzie Love."

"This is Francis Underwood. I'm on my way to the hospital and wondered if you found out anything from your lawyer friend?" Her voice sounded full of fragile hope.

Mac rubbed her forehead where a stabbing pain hit her between the eyes. "I talked to him last night, but I'm afraid the news isn't good."

"What did he say?" Quieter now. On the verge of tears.

"There are no laws against withdrawing life support, but there is a general consensus that a patient should be given at least seventy-two hours before it's considered."

"This morning will be seventy-two hours."

"I know." Mac drew in a breath and let it out. "I asked about any legal issues since Doug is the victim in an ongoing investigation, but there are none. It's up to the doctors."

"So Laura can't just do what she wants?" A note of hope again.

"It's complicated. The family has some say. Yes."

"I see."

Silence filled the air inside the car.

"Francis? Where are you?"

She'd hung up. A shiver went down Mac's spine, and she turned up the heat. At least that phone call was behind her. Now she could get on with her day.

Her phone rang again. Chief Baker.

"Are you still at the hospital?" He asked.

"In the parking lot."

"We've got a problem."

# CHAPTER 22

Panic swelled inside Mac and she couldn't breathe. "Is it Jake?"

"No. Thomas Underwood and Laura James are having a fight in the hallway outside Douglas James's room." He sighed. "Is there any way you could get up there and help contain the situation?"

"On my way." Mac locked her car and hurried across the lot toward the warmth of the hospital lobby once more. Now what? She understood why Francis and Laura were fighting, but Thomas and Laura? What could they be fighting about?

As she stepped off the elevator, their shouts made it all too clear.

"You witch." Thomas's cold words echoed down the hall. "All you care about is the insurance money."

"And all you care about is the business," Laura spat back.

"The business your husband built from the ground up." Thomas poked a finger as close to Laura's face as possible, considering an officer was restraining him. "The business that means everything to him."

A security guard carefully held Laura by the arm, far enough away from Thomas that she couldn't hit or kick him.

"Baloney." She flipped her free hand at him. "You know that if he dies, the business has to be sold. It's a provision in his will. That's all you care about. Then you'll lose your best income stream."

"That's not true." Thomas lunged for her, but the officer planted his feet and managed to resist his forward motion.

"Whoa. You two are enough to wake a man out of a coma." Mac stepped between them and put her hands on her hips.

"Who invited you?" Laura sneered at her.

"The Chief of Police," Mac said, her voice even and calm. "He sent me with a message for you both."

Laura opened her mouth to speak and snapped it shut.

"Mrs. James, the Chief would like you and Mr. Underwood to leave. Take your argument somewhere off hospital grounds, or he will be forced to arrest you for disturbing the peace." She hoped the Chief would be okay with her stretch of what he really said.

"Fine." Laura yanked her arm from the security guard. "Let me get my coat."

"I'll get that for you." Mac ducked into Doug's room and returned with her coat and purse. Thomas Underwood was gone.

"Don't think this will stop me from doing what I think is best for my husband," Laura hissed at Mac.

"I didn't for a moment. Believe me." A sudden tiredness blanketed Mac.

Every time Mac encountered this woman, it was like doing battle. Not just repelling Laura's ugly words, but struggling to hold on to her values. To respond the way she knew she should and not allow herself to fight evil with evil.

In her car once more, Mac replayed the scene in her mind.

Were they play-acting, or was that a real fight? Real. Which meant that Laura and Thomas weren't in on Doug's electrocution. Most likely. She missed the round tables with Sam, Miss P, and Jake. This investigating on her own was for the birds.

And then there was Zoe. Mac needed to find out where Zoe fit into the group. "Arrgh." She felt like her brain was going to explode. It was time to get back to the office and regroup.

The heavy snowfall had stopped, and the sky was lightening. Mac's spirits rose. Jake seemed on the road to recovery. Doug remained on life support. These were all blessings.

So why did she still feel the heaviness in her chest? It lifted a little at the sight of Miss P's sedan parked in the office driveway.

"You're just in time for lunch." Miss P took her coat and hung it on the rack. "I've made vegetable soup."

"Yumm." Mac drank in the aroma permeating the small house that had become a second home to her. "You are amazing."

"It's only soup, my dear." Miss P set a bowl on the table where Mac usually sat. "Would you like iced tea or hot tea?"

"Iced, please."

After a brief blessing, Mac concentrated on letting the warmth of her meal radiate throughout her body. "That was delicious as always." She pushed her bowl to the side and smiled at Miss P.

"Thank you." The older woman pressed her napkin against her mouth. "I take it you saw Detective Sanders this morning. How is he?"

"Jake's good." A different kind of warmth crept up Mac's neck as she remembered their kiss. "I don't think they'll be able to keep him in there much longer."

"I agree. Samantha called a moment before you arrived and told me she was preparing her spare bedroom." Miss P stood and collected the bowls. "She believes her brother will be released today."

"Today?" A spark of pure joy pushed Mac to her feet. "Let me help you." She took the glasses and followed Miss P into the kitchen. Maybe after Jake was home, she'd feel better too.

"What else happened at the hospital?" Miss P faced Mac with raised eyebrows. "I heard a rather strange call on the police band radio."

"Let's put these in the dishwasher and I'll tell you about it."

Mac led the way back to the table with a fresh glass of iced tea. Miss P glided across the floor carrying a brimming cup of hot cocoa. Mac began with finding Laura kissing Jake.

"My, she's what we called a hussy in my day."

Mac chuckled. "That she is." She continued telling her about the woman's determination to stop life support for Doug, and how Mac ended up helping break up a fight between Laura and Thomas Underwood.

"So Mr. Underwood is opposed to turning off the machines as well."

"It seems that way."

"Interesting. For a moment, I thought he may have been in partnership with Mrs. James to kill her husband."

"Me too." Mac pulled a yellow tablet and a pencil over in front of her. "I'm glad you're here. I only wish the whole gang could be sitting around the table."

"I know it's been hard on you—having to investigate on your own."

"It has." Mac couldn't look at her friend or she'd tear up. "I mean, I know you're here. You and Sam. But I miss our interaction. Bouncing ideas off one another."

"This may make you feel better." Miss P looked at her

watch. "Mrs. Green is due here in an hour. I believe Sam is hoping to make it. As well as Zoe."

"Where's Zoe now?" A twinge of guilt pricked Mac. She hadn't missed her old schoolmate.

"She took the files from your parents' case over to Nathaniel." Miss P furrowed her brow. "I expected her back by now."

"You don't think ...?" Mac let the question hang between them.

"I expressed my concerns to you earlier." Miss P entered a number on her phone. "Nathaniel. Where is Miss Dixon? I expected her back at the office some time ago."

*Uh-oh.* Miss P's lips hardened into a grim line. Her friend didn't like whatever Nate was saying.

"I see." The older woman glanced at Mac. "While I'm glad you are making progress on the case, I'm afraid Miss Dixon is needed here. Now."

The last word left no room for discussion.

Miss P pressed End and placed her phone on the table. She took a sip of her hot chocolate and set her mug on a napkin before raising her gaze to Mac. "It seems Nathaniel has been teaching Zoe the finer points of law regarding your parents' case."

"You mean they've been working together on the files." Was she missing something? Why did Miss P seem so angry?

"Mackenzie, I do not believe you understand what a terrible mistake this could be." She clasped her hands on the table. "It's one thing to let Nathaniel be privy to your family's history, and quite another to open it up to Miss Dixon. He already knows most of it."

"What is it about Zoe that worries you?"

"For one, she may be your age, but she lacks your maturity and common sense." Miss P stretched a hand toward Mac. "I am afraid she will not be able to keep the details of your parents' deaths to herself, therefore putting you and possibly your sisters in danger."

Mac rose and paced the room. The problem of Zoe kept getting larger. It came down to trust. Could she trust her friend from high school? Or not? There seemed to be only one way to find out. Mac turned back to Miss P. "I'll have a talk with her, but I'm inclined to let her work with Nate. I've been struggling to figure out where she fits into our organization. Let's see if this helps define her role."

Miss P got to her feet and crossed to Mac. "Your parents would be proud of the wise woman you've become." She placed a hand on Mac's arm. "And I'm proud of you as well."

"Thanks, Miss P." Mac took her friend's hand in hers. "Now, we need to get ready for Mrs. Green's appointment."

"I jotted down a few questions I thought we might want to ask her." Miss P handed her a piece of paper with several lines of elegant writing. "Although it seems you learned the answers to a few of these this morning at the hospital."

"Yes. Thomas Underwood doesn't want Doug dead, and he didn't plan the electrocution with Laura." Mac scanned the list. "You thought of one I didn't."

"Hello, you two." Sam's vibrant voice blew in on the swirl of cold air. "I have good news. Jake is being sprung tonight."

"That *is* good news." Miss P gave a little clap.

"Whoo-hoo." Mac did a fist pump. "When do we pick him up?"

"Not we, girlfriend." Sam threw her coat on a chair. "Alan. We'll meet them at home."

Disappointment arrowed through Mac. She shook it off. Jake was being released, and that was all that mattered.

"What's going on?" The door opened once more, and Zoe hurried in.

"Jake's getting out of the hospital tonight." Sam grabbed Zoe's hands and did a little twirl.

"Okay, ladies, and I use that term loosely, we have a client due here any minute. Get a grip." Visions of Sam falling and ambulance sirens brought Mac's nerves to the brink of meltdown.

"Aye, aye, captain." Sam saluted her and plopped into her desk chair, the one Mac and Miss P insisted she use since she got pregnant. "You need to lighten up a little, my friend."

"Very funny, but while you've been doing whatever you've been doing," Mac waved an arm at her, "I've been trying to solve our case. Alone."

The room went quiet.

"I didn't mean that." Tears stung Mac's eyes as she ran into her office and shut the door.

# CHAPTER 23

Mac buried her face in her hands. Miss P had called her wise. That was some wisdom she showed out there just now. What came over her? She didn't deserve their friendship. Especially Sam.

A knock sounded and the door opened. Sam slipped inside. "Miss P told us what went on today, and about how you've been feeling." She took a seat across the desk. "What I want to know is why you didn't call me?"

"Your brother was in the ICU." Mac grabbed a tissue and blew her nose. "Not to mention ..." She gestured to Sam's belly.

"What? Because I'm pregnant, I can't be your best friend anymore? Because I've got other things I'm dealing with, I don't have time for you?" Sam leaned forward. "Is that how you'd treat me?"

"No." Mac glared at her. "I'd always have time for you."

"Then stop feeling sorry for yourself and give me the same credit."

"Oh, Sam." Mac grabbed another tissue. "Now I feel horrible."

"You should." She leveraged herself out of the chair and walked around the desk. "Here. You missed a little snot." Sam pulled a tissue from the box and wiped Mac's upper lip.

Mac snorted a laugh. "Only you."

"You mean only your best friend?"

"Yeah."

"Don't you ever do that to me again, or I'll name this baby after your middle name."

"You wouldn't do that to your daughter." Mac gasped. "I hate my middle name."

"I would." Sam cocked an eyebrow at her. "Partner. Now, we have a client to interview. You might want to ..." Sam whirled a finger around her face.

"I'll be out in a minute." Mac pulled open the top drawer of her credenza and removed her emergency makeup bag. She closed her eyes. *Forgive me, Lord, for feeling sorry for myself and for not reaching out to Sam for help. Most of all, forgive me for not turning to You first.*

Mac took a deep breath and opened her eyes. The weight was gone. But oh man, did she have some work to do on her face. As she applied the last stroke of lipstick, headlights shone in her windows. Mrs. Green had arrived.

It had only been a matter of days since Mac had seen Ursula Green, but somehow she seemed older, her back more bowed. Maybe it was the parka she wore to protect herself from the cold wind.

"Thank you, sir. You are most kind." Green pressed some bills into the taxi driver's hand.

"No problem, ma'am." He tipped his head. "Call when you're ready to go back home."

"Come in." Miss P stretched a hand out to Mrs. Green. "Thank you for coming out on such a terrible day."

"One day is much the same as another to me." Green

straightened a little and shed her heavy coat. But she kept her hat pulled down on her head. "Hello, everyone." She looked at each of them in turn, pausing on Zoe. "I don't believe we've met."

"No, ma'am." She grinned. "I'm Zoe Dixon. I've only been with the agency for a few months."

Green smiled and nodded. The twinkle in her clear blue eyes seemed to say the woman already knew all she needed about Zoe. Mac wished Mrs. Green would tell her so she'd know too.

"Shall we sit?" Miss P gestured at the large table that served many purposes in their office. "I'll bring us some beverages. Some turmeric and ginger tea for you, Mrs. Green?"

"That would be wonderful." The woman leaned on her cane and began the journey across the floor.

Zoe took a step toward her to help, but Mac caught her eye and motioned her back. Mrs. Green preferred to make her own way.

Once they were all seated, Mac couldn't help but copy Mrs. Green and glance at all her colleagues once more in place around the table. Her heart swelled with thankfulness and gratitude. The only thing that could make it better would be if Jake were here too.

"I assume you have some news for me?" Ursula Green wrapped her hands around her mug and held it close to her face.

"Yes." Mac studied her notes before lifting her gaze. "A lot has happened. I'll try to summarize, and if you have any questions, we can take those after. Okay?"

Green nodded.

"The police now believe that your nephew's electrocution wasn't an accident, but attempted murder. The fuses were switched. Doug thought he was turning off the power to the copier room, but he wasn't."

"Who switched them?"

"We're not sure, but the maintenance man, Zachary Zane, is involved somehow." Mac held up a hand. "There's someone else calling the shots, but we don't know who yet."

"We?" Green set her mug down and stared at Mac.

"Us." Mac indicated herself, Miss P, Sam, and Zoe. "And the police." She leaned on the table. "You should know that several police officers have been injured in the process. Including my fiancé and Sam's brother, Detective Jake Sanders. He and several others were caught in a bomb blast at Zane's sister's home."

Green put her head in her hand. "I'm so sorry. I ..."

"You shouldn't feel guilty. They were doing their job." Mac reached for her. "I just wanted you to know that the police take this very seriously. In fact, Chief Baker would like to speak to you."

"I'll call him." Green lifted her head and nodded. "Anything else?"

"We have a few questions for you that could help us figure out who hurt Doug."

"I'll tell you whatever I can."

"Does Doug have a living will or directive that gives his wishes about life support?"

"I don't know." Her hands shook as she picked up her mug and took a drink of tea. "I believe I have the name of his lawyer at home. I'll look for it."

Mac made a note on her pad. "How about the agreement with his partner, Thomas Underwood?"

"What is it you want to know?"

"My understanding is that if Doug dies, the company is to be sold. Do you know anything about that?"

"No." She shook her head. "Although I wouldn't be surprised. Doug loved—loves—that company, and I think he's beginning to have doubts about Underwood. I could see him not wanting the company to go to either Thomas or Laura."

"The other big question is why a shock from regular household current almost killed your nephew. Any ideas?"

"That is one I can answer." Green's face sagged. "Doug has atrial fibrillation. He was diagnosed five years ago. The doctor encouraged him to stop working, but you know my nephew." She swiped a tear from her cheek. "He told me he would be extra careful."

"How many people knew about his condition?" The hairs on the back of Mac's neck stood up. This could be the break they needed.

"Laura, I imagine. And Thomas."

Mac's excitement lessened.

"Me. His doctor, of course." She furrowed her brow. "I never thought about that. His attacker would have had to know about his AFib." She fixed her clear blue eyes on Mac. "But there's more you're not telling me."

Mac held her gaze. "Mrs. Green, have you been to the hospital to visit Doug?"

"I've tried, but that ... Laura wouldn't let me in. She went so far as to have my name put on the refuse entry list." A flash of anger passed across the woman's face. "Can you believe that? I'm his aunt. His only living blood relative."

"She intends to stop all life support for Doug."

"What?" Green slammed the table with her fists. "Over my dead body." She struggled to rise. "I bet Thomas Underwood is behind this. He's besotted with her."

"Calm down." Mac stood. "Please. Hear me out."

The woman sank back onto her chair.

"Thomas Underwood doesn't want her to do it. Nor does

his sister, Francis. They both had fights with Laura over her plan." Mac eased back down. "For now, your brother is status quo. But, you might want to talk to his doctor and see if you can get another test done for brain activity."

"That will be first on my list." Green blinked away her unfocused stare. "I need to get to the hospital."

"Would you like one of us to go with you?" Mac stood again.

"No. This battle is mine to fight. You keep doing what you're doing." She grasped Mac's hand in hers. "Thank you."

"At least let Zoe or me give you a ride. It will save you a taxi fare."

"No." Mrs. Green slipped an arm into her coat. "I'd rather do this my way if you don't mind."

Zoe held Mrs. Green's coat so she could get her other arm into the sleeve, but the woman wouldn't accept any help zipping it or putting on her gloves. Mac walked her outside where the driver waited on the porch to help her to his taxi.

"We'll keep in touch," Mac said.

The hooded figure nodded once before Mrs. Green climbed into the backseat and the taxi drove away. Lost in thought, Mac stood on the porch until the cold cut through and she shivered.

"Get in here, you fool, it's cold out there." Sam grabbed her arm and yanked her inside.

"I would call that meeting a productive one with the promise of more helpful information." Miss P collected the mugs and turned toward the kitchen at the back of the room.

"Yes, and no." Mac reviewed her notes. "I don't like the idea of Mrs. Green going to the hospital on her own."

"Me either." Sam tapped a few keys and peered at her computer screen. "So, according to my notes, Mrs. Green has agreed to speak to Chief Baker, find the name of Doug's attorney, and talk to his doctor about getting another brain function test done. Is that about it?"

"That's what I've got."

"And she's packing." Zoe brushed crumbs from her blouse.

The other three women stared at her.

She shrugged. "I caught a glimpse of it in her pocket when I helped her on with her coat."

"You're sure it was a gun?" Mac asked.

"Duh." Zoe rolled her eyes. "I know what the barrel of a revolver looks like. Probably a twenty-two."

Oh man. Mac had a bad feeling about this.

# CHAPTER 24

Jake always said Mac had the instincts of a good police officer. Right now, they were screaming at her. She only wished she could interpret what they were saying. "Is it just me, or do any of you feel like something big is about to happen and we haven't been invited?"

"Like a party?" Zoe asked.

"No, not like a party." Mac scowled at her. "Like something bad."

"Oh." Zoe scratched the top of her head where her ponytail started. "I'm not feeling it."

Sam suppressed a smile. "I think you've had a long, hard day already and you're running on pure adrenaline, my friend."

"Even if you're correct, Mackenzie, what can we do except wait for whatever it is to happen?" Miss P folded her hands on the table.

"I hate waiting."

"I know you do, my dear."

"I need to get home to start dinner before Alan and Jake

arrive." Sam shut her computer. "You coming?" She glanced at Mac.

The corners of her mouth turned up in a smile. Jake, home at last. "Yes." Mac stuffed the yellow pad into her bag and scanned the room. "There's nothing here that's urgent. Why don't you two go home as well?"

"Yippee." Zoe sprang to her feet. "David will be pumped."

"I am a bit tired myself." Miss P wound a soft winter scarf around her head before sliding her long black coat over her shoulders.

"Zoe, I'd like to meet with you tomorrow morning here at the office." Mac turned toward the newest member of the agency. "Around nine?"

"Great. See you then." She bounced out the door.

"I will plan on being here also. Before nine." Miss P pulled on her gloves and sighed. "Into the breach once more."

"I'll meet you at your house after I lock up." Mac inclined her head toward Sam. "Be careful on these roads."

"Always." Sam minced her way across the porch and took the steps with care.

Mac shut off the lights, set the alarm, and locked the door. But even as she pulled it shut, an overwhelming feeling of dread washed over her. Something bad was about to happen.

She turned to see Sam safely in her car, driving away, and breathed a sigh of relief. Mimicking Sam's careful steps, Mac got to her sedan and pulled out of the driveway. She caught up with her best friend a few blocks away.

As she followed Sam back to her house, her distress eased. They made it without incident and Alan's car was already there—which meant Jake was there. Her heart leaped in her chest. Maybe her fatigue had her all mixed up and unable to process inner signals correctly. That must be it. She was just tired.

"I guess Alan started dinner." Sam tugged her coat around her belly. "At least I hope so."

"Me too. I'm famished." Mac laughed.

As they reached the door, it opened. Alan ushered them in with a finger to his lips. "Jake's sleeping. They gave him a pill before we brought him home." He pulled Sam in for a kiss. "Hi, Mac."

Mac blinked away sudden tears. What did she expect? That Jake would be standing in the hall with open arms? Make that open arm? She'd have to wait a little longer for the greeting Sam got.

"At least the snow has stopped." Alan peered out the door before shutting it. "Dinner's in the oven. Should be ready in twenty minutes."

"It smells delicious." Mac shed her coat and followed Sam back to the kitchen.

"Yeah, I slaved a long time over it," Alan said.

"Right." Sam laughed. "Frozen lasagna and garlic bread out of the box." She kissed him on the cheek. "But thank you for getting it ready. I love you."

"Love you more." Alan pointed to the stove. "Keep an eye on the time. I'll go rouse Jake."

Mac straightened the silverware, her gaze focused on the doorway into the kitchen. "It seems like forever since we were all here together."

"I know." Sam pulled on two oven mitts. "I'm so hungry I could eat this lasagna by myself."

"You'd regret it later."

At the sound of Jake's low voice, joy shot through Mac, and she hurried toward him. He threw his good arm around her, pulled her close, and she got the kiss she'd been waiting for.

"Now, I'm ready to eat." Jake grinned at her. "I might need a little help cutting my food."

"I think that can be arranged." Mac led the way to the table.

Alan handed out large pieces of steaming lasagna and placed a basket of garlic bread on the table. Mac helped Sam with glasses of water. Alan blessed the meal, adding a special thanks for Jake.

"Amen." Mac lifted her own silent prayer of thanksgiving for the three people with her at the table. Especially the guy with the sandy blond hair and blue-gray eyes who struggled to cut his lasagna with his fork. "Let me help." She leaned over.

"Thanks," he murmured in her ear. "I'll pay you back later."

"Much later, from the look of you." She threw him a haughty look.

"Ouch." He placed his free hand over his heart in feigned pain. "Way to hurt a guy."

"You need to concentrate on getting better." Mac brandished the knife at him. "That's your job for the time being."

"Yes, boss."

"Will you two stop playing around and eat?" Sam used her best mom-to-be voice. "Or I'll be forced to separate you."

"You will be an excellent mother." Mac grinned at her. Life was back to normal. She glanced at Jake. Well, almost back.

The savory Italian baked meal-in-one with pasta, cheese, and red sauce melted in her mouth. Food never tasted so good. And the garlic bread—yummy. Mac hadn't realized how hungry she was.

In the midst of enjoying her second piece of bread, the doorbell chimed. She started to rise before remembering this wasn't her house.

Alan returned with a man with warm brown skin. "Detective Walker is here."

"Hi, Walker." Jake pushed to his feet and extended his hand. "Good to see you."

"You too, Jake." His deep brown eyes sparkled above his broad smile. He clasped Jake's hand in his. "We've been praying for you, man. Looking forward to having you back with us."

"I can't wait to be back." Jake released Walker's hand. "Pull up a chair."

He shook his head. "I came on an errand for the Chief."

"What does he want from me now?" Jake chuckled. "I'm not good for much, but my brain still works."

"It's not you he wants." Walker rubbed the bridge of his nose and cut his eyes to Mac. "It's Ms. Love."

# CHAPTER 25

"The Chief wants to see me?" Mac bolted to her feet. "Why?"

Detective Walker hesitated, scanning the faces of the others. "I'm not sure he'd want me to ..."

Jake turned to face her, his eyes dark with suppressed questions—and hurt.

"You can speak freely here, Detective." She stepped over to Jake and touched his hand with hers.

Walker rubbed the back of his neck. "The Chief wants me to deputize you and bring you to a crime scene at the hospital."

"Deputize her?" Jake stiffened. "No way ..." He gulped back the words and passed his hand over his forehead. "Sorry."

Walker gave her a pleading look. "Could we go, please?"

Was this the bad thing that plagued Mac all day? What should she do? It was clear Jake didn't want her to go, but this was a request from the Chief. His boss. And she'd been working with him a couple of days now while Jake lay in a hospital bed. "Can you give me a couple of minutes, Detective Walker?"

He nodded and strolled off.

Alan and Sam left the room.

"I know you're upset." Mac faced Jake. "All you care about is keeping me safe. But we talked about this before. Remember?"

"That was before we were engaged." His gaze gripped hers. "I don't know why, but that makes a difference. I know logically it shouldn't, but it does. In here." He tapped his heart.

"But you trust me."

"Of course."

"While you've been in the hospital, I've been working with Chief Baker to try to find out who's responsible for electrocuting Doug. Sam knows the whole story, and she can bring you up to speed." Mac took his hand in hers. "I have to see this through. This is my case too."

"I get it." He drew her to him and kissed her hair. "I don't like it, but that's something I need to work on." He released her. "But I want to know what's going on."

"I promise to let you know as soon as I can."

"You'd better go. Walker is waiting."

"I love you, Jake Sanders."

"I love you more, Deputy Love."

Deputy Love. Yikes. She grabbed her coat and purse. "I'll be back later." She hoped.

"Do you want to ride with me or drive yourself?" Walker asked.

"I'll follow you. That way, if you need to stay, I can leave early." She looked at him. "So when do I get deputized?"

"You just did." He grinned at her. "We need to get back." He opened the car door for her.

"What happened?" Mac hopped behind the wheel and looked up at the detective.

"Laura James has been murdered."

A chill skittered down her spine that had nothing to do

with the temperature outside, but she upped the heat anyway. Questions poured into her brain like water from a firehose, and she wished she'd ridden with Detective Walker after all. Now she'd have to plug the dam until she got to the hospital.

Lights with generators lit up the crime scene in the hospital parking lot. One question answered. Laura James had been killed in her car. Mac pulled up her jacket's hood and strode over to where the Chief stood with a couple of other officers.

"Good. You're here." Chief Baker motioned for her to follow him. A large white tent had been erected around a small sedan. Generators provided heat to keep it warm enough inside for the forensics team to work. "The guard found her about an hour ago. She's been shot in the head."

Mac steeled herself. She'd seen a man whose throat had been cut, and that was gruesome enough, but never someone shot in the head. The Chief raised the flap of the tent and gestured her inside. Laura's body was gone. She sighed with relief.

"Thought you were going to see a dead body again, didn't you?" The Chief patted her on the shoulder. "I wouldn't do that to you. Bad enough you were first on the scene for my brother."

"Thanks for that."

"I wanted you to see the scene, though. You see things we don't. I appreciate that."

Mac shot a prayer to heaven for guidance and clarity of vision before focusing on the car and its surroundings. Too many feet had trampled the snow around the car to be of any help. Although ... Was she seeing a woman's boot print? "Can I use your flashlight?"

"Sure."

Mac squatted and angled the light on an area of the snow

she hadn't walked on. "Any women on your team or with the forensics people? And would they be wearing snow boots?"

"There's a couple. They'd wear regulation-issued boots. Why?"

"I'm seeing a print over here you might want to check out." Mac indicated where she was looking.

The Chief called out to his team, and someone came in and marked the area.

"She knew her killer." Mac stood next to the Chief. "She wouldn't roll her window down for just anyone."

"Yeah. It looks to be a twenty-two revolver. We didn't find any shells."

Mac's hands curled into fists. A revolver like Mrs. Green carried in her coat pocket? She raised her gaze to the front seat of the car. "Where's all the blood and ... other stuff?"

"That's the other reason we think it had to be a twenty-two. The bullets went in, but didn't come out."

Mac swallowed the bile that image conjured in her brain. "You said bullets. How many shots were there?"

"The M.E. counted three entry holes."

In her mind, she visualized Mrs. Green approaching the car. "She must have tapped on the window, waited for Laura to lower it, pulled the gun, and shot her. No hesitation."

"Who?"

Mac shifted her gaze to Chief Baker.

"You said she. Who do you think did this?"

Mac shook her head. She needed time to think. Time to check before she accused anyone—especially her client. "Nobody in particular. I don't know why I said she. It could have been a man."

"Do you have any idea who'd want Laura James dead?"

Three names sprang into her mind. "I can think of a couple

of people who hate her, but neither of them seems like the killing type. And I'm not sure their reasons would lead them to do this." She gestured toward the car.

"Let me be the judge of that." The Chief lifted the flap of the tent. "Let's find a warmer place to talk." He led her to the patrol car he'd left running.

She melted into the seat and closed her eyes for a moment. Warm air poured onto her feet.

"Thomas Underwood is already at the top of my list." The Chief's gruff voice cut through the air. "Who else would you add?"

"Francis Underwood, his sister." She shifted in her seat. "But I can't see either of them as killers."

"We have to start somewhere." He made a note in his book and narrowed his gaze at her. "Who else?"

She averted her gaze for a moment. The title of deputy brought responsibility with it that she wasn't used to. "I told you we've been working with Doug's aunt, Mrs. Green. Earlier today, we told her that Laura was going to stop the life support to her nephew, and she got very angry."

"Angry enough to confront Mrs. James?"

"I think so." Mac licked her lips. "And we know she had a revolver in her coat pocket when she left the office."

"Okay." He picked up the mic and issued an All-Points Bulletin for Mrs. Green. Possibly armed and dangerous.

Trapped between guilt and duty, Mac prayed for a miracle. "I'm not sure I like this deputy stuff."

Chief Baker turned sorrow-filled eyes on her. "It's not an easy job, but I appreciate your help. Why don't you go home, and we'll talk more in the morning."

Mac gave him a small smile and climbed out of his vehicle. The chill air hit her in the face, forcing her to lower her head as she walked to her car. As she reached for the handle, a figure in a hooded parka bumped into her and pinned her against her sedan.

# CHAPTER 26

Adrenaline surged through her. Mac inched her gloved hand inside her purse, searching for her pepper spray.

"I warned you once to forget the past," a husky whisper sounded in her ear, "but you didn't listen. You got your lawyer friend involved. Now he's in danger too. Stop now or you'll both regret it."

The pressing bulk released her. Mac swiveled, spray in hand, to see the figure disappear between the cars. Frustration and anger boiled inside her until it exploded in a scream. Three officers, including Detective Walker, rushed across the lot to her.

"What happened? Are you okay?"

Embarrassment warmed her cheeks, and she was thankful for the shadows. "A man accosted me. He ran off that way." Mac pointed into the darkness.

"What was he wearing?"

"A hooded parka." She circled her face. "With a scarf covering his face."

Two officers sprinted in the direction Mac had indicated.

"Did he say anything?" Walker asked.

She wasn't up to explaining the first threat and the reason behind it. "He mumbled something. I didn't get it."

"Why did he run?"

"I don't know." Mac shrugged. "Maybe he saw all the police in the lot and was worried I'd scream." Which might have been true if this were a normal mugging. But it wasn't.

"Okay." Walker tilted his head at her. He flipped his book closed. "If you think of anything else, call me. Would you like me to follow you back to Sam's house?"

"No. I think I'll go on home." Mac unlocked her car and climbed in. "Thanks."

"No problem." He gave her a grim smile. "Be safe."

"Always." While the heater warmed up, Mac dialed Jake's number. It went to voicemail. She tried Sam.

"Hi. Are you okay?" Sam's soft voice filled the car.

"Yeah. I guess Jake's asleep?"

"He passed out about an hour ago. He said to wake him if you called, but ..."

"No." Mac yawned. "I'll talk to him in the morning."

"What happened at the hospital? Are you able to talk about it?"

"Laura James was shot in her car. With a twenty-two revolver." Mac waited for the last bit of information to click with Sam.

"Like the one Zoe saw in Mrs. Green's pocket?" Sam's tone lifted a notch.

"I believe so. I had to tell the Chief, and I feel terrible. What if the poor woman had nothing to do with it?"

"Mac, what if she did? You can't withhold information based on whether you like someone or not."

"No." Fatigue washed over Mac. "I'm going home to get

some sleep. I have an appointment with Zoe in the morning at the office, and then I'll be by."

"Sleep well, my friend."

"You too."

To Mac's surprise, after the evening she'd had, she slept like a hibernating bear and almost didn't hear her alarm go off. She awoke refreshed, and after a quick shower and breakfast, she was on the road. It was ten minutes to nine when she pulled into the office driveway.

"Good morning, Mackenzie." Miss P placed a plate of freshly baked cinnamon rolls on the office table. "Have you had breakfast?"

"I have, but I always have room for one of your pastries." Mac chose one on the edge and gingerly picked it up between her thumb and first finger. "Uhmmm." She swallowed and wiped her mouth. "Now I'm ready to face the day."

She placed it on a plate and licked her fingers. "Let me know when Zoe arrives. I'll be in my office."

"Of course." Mrs. P sat at the table and pulled a file in front of her.

At ten after nine, Mac stared at her office door. Part of what she intended to speak to Zoe about was being on time. She picked up her phone to call the woman.

"Sorry." Zoe's muffled voice sounded through Mac's door. "I couldn't get my car started."

Mac replaced her phone on the desk.

"Wait here a moment. I'll let Ms. Love know you're here." Miss P tapped on the door and opened it a foot. "Zoe has arrived."

"I heard. Send her in."

Zoe's entrance was somewhat subdued. She cast a quizzical look at Mac. "Ms. Love? Am I being called on the carpet?"

"In a way." Mac tilted her head back and forth. "I think we need to talk about your place in the agency. Why don't you sit down and tell me what you see as your role here?"

"Hmm." Zoe scrunched up her brow in thought. "I never saw myself as having a 'role.'" She air-quoted the last word. "I just do what you tell me to do. I guess I'd call myself a girl Friday if anything."

"How are you with computers?"

"Not great. Nothing like Sam."

"What about research?"

"Oh, Miss P is amazing. I've learned so much from her."

"What do you see as your strengths or talents?"

"I'm a people person. I've got a positive outlook on life. I'm ready to help in any way I can." She raised a finger. "And Nate says I'm a quick learner. At least when it comes to legal stuff. Maybe that's my role."

Nate. Mac groaned inside. "I'm thinking about allowing you to continue to work with him."

"Cool."

"I haven't decided for sure yet." Mac raised an eyebrow at her former high school friend. "The case, as you know, involves my parents' deaths, and there are facts that must be kept very confidential. Nate has been privy to these details for years, and I know I can trust him." Mac paused. "The question is, can I trust you with my family secrets?"

"Mac." Zoe placed a hand over her heart. "I promise you. I would never tell anyone about a case. Especially one involving you and your family. I take my work here very seriously."

Mac searched the woman's face for any sign of falsehood or weakness. She found none. "The other aspect of the case that I need to make you aware of is that I've received two threats warning me off looking into my parents' murders. One was directed at me only, but the latest included Nate."

Zoe gasped.

"I haven't talked to him about it yet, so I'm asking you not to say anything until I've had a chance." Mac rubbed the bridge of her nose. "If I allow you to work with Nate, I feel like I'm placing you in danger as well, and I'm not sure I can live with that."

"Do I have a say in the decision?"

Mac met Zoe's fierce gaze. "I'm listening."

"I want to work on the case. No matter the risk." Zoe's beautiful face hardened. "You can trust me, Mac. I've had to learn to be joyful in all circumstances—like the Good Book says—but that joy came at a high price. Underneath the fluff is granite."

"I sensed it was there." Mac sighed. "I have a feeling we're going to need to see more of the granite in the future. Can you do that?"

"Yes." Her expression softened into a smile.

Miss P tapped on the door before opening it. "Nathaniel is on the phone, and he sounds very excited." She approached the desk.

Mac picked up the receiver. "Nate. Glad you called. I was—"

"Get out of here." A loud crash sounded on the other end before the line went dead.

# CHAPTER 27

Breath-pinching fear delayed Mac's response. Zoe yanked her cellphone from her pocket and punched three numbers, but before her call went through, the receiver in Mac's hand shrilled to life. Mac punched the call button while Zoe pressed End.

"Sorry." Nate's irritated voice sounded over the speaker. "Aunt P's bird came out of nowhere and dive-bombed me. I dropped the phone."

Miss P took the phone from Mac. "I'm sorry, Nathaniel. I intended to put Cupric back in his cage before I left. I hope he didn't hurt you?"

"No, but I dumped my notes on the floor trying to get out of his way." Nate growled a few words about roasted parakeet.

Mac paced over to her window and waited for her nerves to calm. That had brought it all home for her. She had no right to drag anyone else into her search for her parents' killer. It was too dangerous. She turned and motioned for Miss P to hand her the phone.

"I've discovered some things about your parents' dealings

with Quinton Underwood and Oliver DeLuca." Nate shuffled papers on his end.

"I want you to stop now." Mac's tone cut like a surgical knife. With a sharp, clean edge. "It's too dangerous. Miss P will retrieve the files."

"No." His voice turned to stone. "I want to do this. I need to do this."

"Didn't you hear me?" She was yelling now. "A man accosted me in the hospital parking lot. He said in no uncertain terms that you're in danger too." She pressed a hand to her forehead. "I can't let you risk your life for my problem."

"I'll take precautions, but I'm keeping the files. I'm going to help you. But don't send Zoe over. She's ... I don't want her to get hurt."

The line went dead.

"If Nate's staying on the case, I'm staying on it too." Zoe strode forward. "We talked about this."

"I'm trying to keep you both safe." Mac spit the words out between clenched teeth. "Why are you making this so hard?"

"Maybe for the same reason you get so mad at Jake when he tries to protect you?" Zoe shifted her gaze from Mac to Miss P. "We're in this together. You need us, and we need you."

Heat climbed from under Mac's collar up her neck to her cheeks. Zoe had gone too far. How dare she compare what she was doing to what Jake had done to her? The two things were entirely different.

"Come along, Zoe, my dear." Miss P opened the office door. "I believe Mackenzie needs some time alone."

Mac marched in circles around her desk. It was a bad decision to hire her old classmate, and an even worse one to ask her old boyfriend to help with her parents' case. Then to put them together. She threw up her hands. What had she been thinking?

A photo of her parents stood on her bookcase. They stood, arms linked, in front of their store with big smiles on both their faces. A blanket of fatigue settled on Mac's shoulders, pulling them down. How would she possibly make sense of all the legal documents without Nate's help? She was convinced that was where the clue to their killer lay.

And with Sam in the last trimester of her pregnancy, Mac needed Zoe to help with the physical demands of the agency. She plopped into her chair. Now she understood where Jake was coming from. She still didn't like it, but she understood it.

Mac pushed to her feet and took a deep breath. Time to apologize for her earlier behavior. She stepped into the reception area. "Zoe, you're right. I'm treating you the same way Jake treated me."

"Does this mean I can continue to work on your parents' case?"

"Yes." Mac prayed she wouldn't regret it.

"Thank you." The buxom woman threw her arms around Mac in a quick hug. "You won't be sorry. I've been talking to Nate, and he's making progress. With any luck, we'll have news for you later today."

"Stay alert." Mac fixed her with a no-nonsense look. "I mean it."

"I carry my gun in my waistband now." Zoe lifted her shirt to show Mac. "I'm a good shot."

"Just don't let Nate touch it. He's an ex-con, remember? If he's caught in possession of a gun, it's back to prison for him."

"I haven't told him I have it."

"Good. Don't." After Zoe left, Mac turned to Miss P. "What are your plans for today?"

"I'm helping Samantha take care of Detective Sanders."

"I'm headed over there too. Maybe we'll move our

operations to Sam's house for the time being. That way, Jake can be in on it too."

"Excellent idea." Miss P straightened the collar of her coat. "Shall we close up here?"

"Let me get a few things. Then we can go." Mac grabbed her jacket on the way through the doorway into her office. Foreboding slammed into her like a brick wall. "Now what?" she asked the familiar surroundings.

But when there was no answer, she moved to her desk and retrieved the files she needed. She'd have to deal with whatever was about to happen when it happened. What choice did she have?

As Mac pulled the front door shut, she uttered a prayer of protection over the offices of Mackenzie Love and Samantha Majors, Private Investigators.

"Shall I follow you to Samantha's house?" Miss P pulled on her gloves.

"That's fine." Mac got in her car and backed out of the driveway.

The streets were clear of snow, and fifteen minutes later, the two women stood on Sam's porch.

Killer greeted them with snarly goldendoodle smiles that made him sneeze.

"Good to see you, boy." Mac gave his head a vigorous rub with both hands. She kept far enough away to avoid his doggie kisses.

Done greeting Mac, Killer headed for Miss P.

"Sit," Miss P said in the teacher voice she'd perfected over the years.

The squirming dog plopped his rear down instantly.

"Stay." Miss P held up one finger.

The dog looked at her with adoring eyes.

"Good dog." She smiled at him and stroked his head.

"She's the only one who can get him to do that." Sam shook her head. "I don't understand it."

"I believe you should be able to as well." Miss P glanced at her. "You already sound like a mother at times. That's the tone to use with Killer."

"I'll try it." Sam chuckled.

Jake stuck his head around the corner. "Are you ladies joining me, or are we meeting in the foyer?"

Killer took off down the hall toward a new playmate.

The aroma of vegetable soup drew Mac to the stove. She lifted the lid on a large pot and inhaled. "This smells so good."

"It's for lunch. I figured you and Miss P might be joining us, and I think Alan's going to try to get home too." Sam stepped next to her.

"Is it okay if we make this our office for now?" Mac hip bumped her friend.

"I was hoping you would. I hate being out of the loop." Sam glanced over her shoulder at her brother. "And I know Jake would love to know what's going on."

Mac turned. "I miss working with him."

"It won't be long." Sam placed a hand on Mac's shoulder. "In the meantime, let's sit down and get caught up."

Mac circled the table to sit next to Jake. She kissed him on top of his head. "Good to see you."

"You too." He brought her hand to his lips. "Sam told me what happened last night and about Mrs. Green."

Mac nodded. "I can't believe she killed Laura James." She sat and pulled a yellow pad out of her bag. "But right now, she's the one with opportunity, means, and motive."

"The three things necessary for murder." He ran a hand through his hair. "Are there any other possible suspects?"

"Both Thomas Underwood and his sister, Francis, argued with Laura about stopping the life support for Doug." Mac scribbled on her pad. "Which would be the same motive as Mrs. Green."

"Do you know where they were last evening?"

"Not yet, but that's high on my list of things to check on. Along with whether either of them owns a twenty-two revolver." Mac looked at Sam. "Would you and Miss P look into the gun ownership issue?"

"On it." Sam tapped some keys on her computer.

"I'd also like you to find out where Quinton Underwood and Oliver DeLuca are now."

"Who are they?" Jake gave her a quizzical look. "Are they involved in this case?"

"No. They're part of my parents' murder case." She cut her eyes to Miss P. Sam and Jake didn't know about the second threat. And she wasn't looking forward to Jake's reaction.

"Mac, what aren't you telling me?" Jake leaned into her personal space.

She tapped him on the nose and grinned.

"That won't work."

"Back off a little and I'll tell you." She gave him a gentle shove. The words about her attack came out in a rush. "But, I'm fine. It was only another threat. Nate and Zoe know about it and they insist on continuing to work on the case."

Jake closed his eyes and pinched the bridge of his nose.

She thought she heard murmured counting but couldn't be sure.

"I hate this." He slapped his left shoulder and winced. "You shouldn't be out there on your own. I'm telling the Chief to get you police escorts."

"Jake, they're already thin after the bombing." Mac scooted her chair around to face him. "I'll be more careful. Promise."

"When do you start rehabilitation on your shoulder?" Miss P asked.

"Today. Alan is doing it." Jake shifted his gaze to her.

"And how long will it take?"

"In about a week, I should be able to go back to work on desk duty." Jake straightened. "It will take another month until I can be active again."

"You're fortunate your injury will not keep you from permanently doing your job, Detective Sanders." She peered at him over her glasses.

"Yes, ma'am."

Leave it to Miss P to put things in perspective. "Now. Can we get back to business?" Mac shuffled some papers. "After lunch, I'll pick up Zoe and we'll go see Francis and Thomas Underwood."

Miss P stepped away from the group and put her phone to her ear. When she finished her call, the look of urgency on her face brought back the earlier feeling of unease for Mac. "What's wrong?"

"I spoke to Nathaniel. It seems Zoe never made it to the house."

# CHAPTER 28

A whisper of alarm shot through Mac. "We need to find her."

"She did say she had car trouble on the way to work this morning." Miss P passed a hand across her forehead. "Possibly that is the reason."

"Phone her." Mac jumped up and grabbed her coat.

"No answer," Sam said.

"I'll get ahold of the Chief." Jake picked up his phone.

Mac headed for the door. "Let me know if she calls."

"Mac, I'll come with you." Sam slung her purse over her shoulder and her jacket over her arm. "Don't try to talk me out of it."

Joy zipped through Mac. She and Sam on a case together once more. But then her gaze took in Sam's belly and a moment of panic made her hands shake. She hesitated at the car.

"Unlock the door." Sam glared at her. "It's cold out here."

Mac sighed and did as she was told.

"What route would she have taken?" Sam pushed the seat back as far as it would go and pulled the seatbelt over her big stomach.

"It's pretty straightforward from the office to Miss P's house. Unless Zoe had an errand to run." Mac turned south on Olive. "Is that her Jeep on the right?"

"Looks like it." Sam peered ahead. "It's been hit."

Mac pulled to the curb, hopped out, and hurried to the driver's side window. Zoe was slumped over the steering wheel. "Sam, call an ambulance. Zoe's hurt."

Mac tried the door. It was jammed. "Zoe." She banged on the window. No response. She ran around to the passenger side, yanked the car door open, and leaned in. "Zoe, can you hear me?"

"Ouch." Zoe lifted her head and placed a hand on her forehead. "I'm bleeding." She stared at her red-stained fingers.

"I've called an ambulance. Sit still." Mac gave Sam a thumbs-up to let her know Zoe was awake. "What happened?"

"Some bozo ran into me." She swiveled her head. "Where is the brain-dead truck jockey? I'd like to have a little talk with him."

"He's not here." Mac would like a few words with him too. "It was a hit-and-run. Do you remember what—"

An ambulance screamed to a halt in the middle of the street and two emergency medical personnel jumped out. A squad car followed behind.

Mac backed out of the sports utility vehicle. "I couldn't get the driver's door open."

"We'll see what we can do." They brought out big pliers and worked it open.

Mac walked back to her sedan, where Sam was on the phone.

"Here's Mac. You can speak to her." She handed it to Mac. "It's Miss P."

"I think she's okay. Just upset she can't give the guy who hit her a piece of her mind."

"Did she get a look at the car or truck—I would suppose it had to be a truck or SUV—that hit her?"

"I was about to ask her when the ambulance got here." Along with a few other questions. But they'd have to wait.

One of the EMTs approached Mac's car. "Ma'am, Ms. Dixon is refusing medical attention. She insists she's fine and wants to speak to you."

"Of course she is." Mac climbed out of her car once more.

"It's just a bump on the head." Zoe waved a hand at the bandage across her forehead. "Why take up their valuable time, and the hospital's, for nothing?"

How many times had Mac spoken those same words to Sam, or Jake, or Miss P? "Okay. I'll accept responsibility for her." Mac glared at Zoe. "But you're not driving your car. It's evidence." She turned to the officers nearby. "Can you arrange to have it towed to the police garage?" Mac flashed her credentials.

"Yes, ma'am."

"Did you get a statement?"

The one officer nodded. "Hope you feel better, Ms. Dixon."

Zoe grimaced. "I've got a splitting headache."

"Didn't they give you anything?" Mac asked.

"Acetaminophen." She rolled her eyes and winced. "You got anything stronger?"

"Ibuprofen."

"Great. Can I have a couple?"

"Sure. Get in the car."

"Zoe, how are you?" Sam swiveled in her seat, a look of concern on her face. "We were so worried about you."

"Thanks. It was pretty wild. This truck came out of nowhere." Zoe leaned forward between the seats. "I promise I was watching for anyone following me, and there was no one. When all of a sudden my rearview mirror lit up with the brights of a truck right on my bumper. I have no idea where he came from."

"Could you tell what make of truck it was?" Mac asked.

"Not the make, but from the headlights, I'd say it was a newer model pickup." Zoe chewed her lip in thought. "A big one that had been jacked up."

"How do you know all that?" Sam asked.

"I grew up around cars and trucks." Zoe sat back and closed her eyes.

What Mac knew Zoe wasn't telling Sam was that her dad and her uncle ran a chop shop. They would buy stolen cars and trucks, take them apart, and sell the parts. Until they were caught. By then, Zoe was married and had moved away.

Her mom and dad divorced, and when her dad got out of prison, he moved across the country. Her sister and mom still lived in Washington.

"Did you see a color?" Mac got no answer. Either Zoe had fallen asleep or she feigned sleep to avoid Sam's questions. Either way, it was okay. Mac could ask her later.

Sam cut her eyes to Mac in a questioning gaze.

"Later," Mac mouthed. Aloud, she said, "I'll drop you at your house, and if Zoe's up to it, we'll find Francis and Thomas for a few questions about their whereabouts last evening."

Light snoring reached Mac from the backseat, and Sam slumped against the passenger door. Both women were asleep. The car bumped over the slight incline into Sam's driveway and Mac caught sight of Zoe's yawn in the rearview mirror. Sam straightened and blinked.

Mac sighed. Neither of her friends was in any shape to

interview suspected murderers. She was on her own again. "We're home. Everybody out."

"I thought you were going to drop me and go on." Sam looked at her.

Mac inclined her head toward Zoe, who had fallen asleep again. "I need to take her home."

"Then you might as well come in and have lunch. Zoe can rest on the couch."

Between them, they woke the third woman enough to get her inside and settled on the sofa. Over a lunch of soup and bread, Mac and Sam told Jake and Miss P about Zoe's accident.

"The police are towing her car to the lot where forensics can go over it." Jake swiped at a spot of soup on his shirt. "I always manage to wear my meal."

"I hope you're good at laundry," Mac smirked at him.

"Wait a minute." He pretended to be shocked. "I thought clothes washing fell under your job description."

"You didn't read the fine print. Not if there are excessive stains."

"The fine print will get you every time, my friend." Alan laughed.

"Speaking of fine print, I found out that Thomas Underwood owns a twenty-two revolver." Sam stood and carried her bowl to the sink. "And that he and Francis are regulars at the gun range."

"Good work, Sam." Mac stacked Jake's bowl and hers together. "Now, if I can find out if they were still at the hospital when Laura was shot, we can add them to the suspect list."

"You really don't think Mrs. Green did it, do you?" Jake asked.

Mac stopped. "I don't. It's a feeling."

"Be careful, Mac. Those feelings aren't always right." Jake touched her arm. "I know from experience."

Her phone vibrated in her pocket. Chief Baker wanted her to call. She stepped into the foyer and pressed his number. "Hi, Chief. What's up?"

"We've brought Mrs. Green in for questioning, but she won't talk without you, Sam, and Miss P present."

# CHAPTER 29

Mac gazed back at the kitchen. "I'm not sure all three of us can come, but let me check and call you back." A heaviness invaded her spirit. Mrs. Green couldn't have killed Laura, could she? She walked back to the kitchen. "Alan, are you going to be here with Jake this afternoon?"

"Yes. We're starting his physical therapy. Why?"

"Would it be all right if Sam, Miss P, and I went to the police station for a while? Mrs. Green is in custody, and she wants to speak to us."

"That's fine. Jake and I have work to do." Alan glanced at Zoe passed out on the sofa. "And she looks comfortable."

Mac turned her gaze on Jake. "I guess I'll find out if I can trust my feelings."

He wrapped his good arm around her. "Even if you got this one wrong, don't give up on your inner voice. Most times it will be right."

"I love you, Jake Sanders."

"Love you more, Mac." He leaned down and kissed her. "See you later."

Mac pressed redial. "Chief, we're on our way."

M AC, Sam, and Miss P took the elevator to the police department, located on the second floor of the Public Safety building. Chief Baker and Detective Walker met them in the lobby.

"We've arranged for you ladies to speak with Mrs. Green for five minutes." Chief Baker preceded them down the hall, glancing back over his shoulder to speak. "Then Detective Walker will conduct the formal interview." He stopped at a door labeled Interview Room One. "Five minutes." He peeked through a narrow window in the door. Satisfied, he ushered them inside and left.

Mrs. Green sat bent over on a white plastic chair along the left wall. Mac indicated that Sam should take the rolling chair and Miss P the other plastic chair. She perched on the corner of the desk.

"Thank you for coming." Mrs. Green raised her head. "First, I did not kill Laura even though I felt like it after what you told me." She shook her head.

"Did you go to the hospital when you left us?" Mac asked.

"I did. I went in search of Doug's doctor."

"And?"

"I eventually found him, and he agreed that another test was needed before anything drastic should be done."

"What did you do then?"

"I left. I intended to go home and try to find the name of Doug's lawyer, but as I was walking across the lot, I spotted Laura's car. It was running and it looked like she was sitting in it." She passed a shaky hand across her forehead. "I made a big mistake."

Mac's breath snagged in her throat.

"What did you do, Mrs. Green?" Miss P asked.

"I went over to Laura's car. I wanted to tell her what the doctor had said, and that I was going to get in touch with Doug's lawyer."

"What happened when you spoke with her?"

Mac got up and walked to the corner of the room as if she could distance herself from what she was about to hear. She resisted the urge to plug her ears with her fingers.

"I didn't get the chance. She was already dead." Mrs. Green began to tremble. "I've never seen a murdered person before. It was terrible."

"Laura was dead?" Mac strode toward her. "Do you know what time this was?"

"You believe me?" Mrs. Green raised eyes filled with hope.

"I do." Mac took her hand. "But it would help if you could tell us what— "

The door opened. "Sorry, ladies. Time's up."

"Six-thirty." The sound of Mrs. Green's voice followed them into the hall.

Mac stopped Detective Walker as he approached the door. "She didn't do it. She did see Laura after she'd been killed. I think soon after. You'll want to ask her about what else she saw around that time."

"Thanks, Mac, but I think I'll conduct my own interview." Walker gave her an indulgent smile. "I like to form my own opinions."

"Yeah." She stuffed her hands in her pockets. "Of course. I was just trying to help."

"And I appreciate it. Tell Jake hello."

Which meant 'move along, Mac.' Whatever happened to Deputy Love?

"How did it go?" The Chief caught up to them in the foyer.

"Thanks for letting us talk to her." Mac chewed on her lip. "I told Detective Walker what we learned."

"Oh." He narrowed his eyes at her. "Everything okay?"

"Sure." She flashed a smile at him and turned to go. At the elevator, she pivoted and took a couple of steps back his way. "Am I still deputized?"

"As far as I'm concerned."

"Then why couldn't I sit in on the interview, and why is Walker treating me like I'm a thorn in his side?"

"As for sitting in on the interview, I deputized you to help with the crime scene as an investigator. Your duties would not extend to interviewing suspects. As for Walker's attitude, I have no idea." He shrugged. "But I still need your help for investigating if you're willing."

"I am." His answer made sense. She was a private investigator. As Sam always said, she had skills. "Please let me know if you charge Mrs. Green."

"I will."

Sam and Miss P waited in the downstairs foyer.

"What was that all about?" Sam asked.

"I was clarifying my role as a deputy."

"Mac, you're always pushing the boundaries." Sam eased herself into the front passenger's seat.

"I suppose I am." Was that a bad thing or a good thing?

"Let's get back and see how our two patients are doing," Miss P said. "I would imagine Alan is ready for some help by now."

Mac's four-door sedan had barely come to a stop before Alan was out the door and helping Sam with her car door.

"Boy, am I glad to see you." He pulled her in for a hug.

"That bad, huh?" Sam chuckled.

"Nice woman, but man, can she talk." He glanced over his shoulder. "She's not behind me, is she?"

"How's Jake?" Mac led the way up the sidewalk to the porch.

"He's sleeping. I put him through quite a workout." Alan held the front door for the women. "He'll probably be sore when he wakes up. Muscle soreness, not angry. At least I hope he's not angry with me."

"Silly." Sam slapped her husband's well-muscled arm. "He's happy you can do his therapy and he doesn't have to go to a stranger."

"Yeah, well. We'll see how he feels after a few sessions." Alan snatched his jacket from the chair. "I need to go. See you later."

"Bye, Alan." Zoe waved at him. "It was nice talking to you."

He lifted his chin in her direction before disappearing through the door.

"Your husband is so nice." Zoe gave Sam a big smile.

"Yes, he is." Sam sat at the table and opened her computer.

Miss P retrieved her files and checked her email on her phone. Mac pulled out a chair and placed a yellow pad and pencil in front of her. She motioned for Zoe to sit.

"Let's go back to the beginning." Mac made a note on her pad. "Doug's accident that turned out not to be an accident."

"Do we still believe Laura was responsible for convincing Zane to switch the fuses?" Miss P asked.

"What do you think?" Mac scanned the faces around the table.

"Why not?" Zoe shrugged. "She has the best motive. Insurance money, and she gets part of the company if he dies. And she knew the shock could kill him because of his heart condition."

"Yes, but she also knew that Douglas's will stipulated that upon his death, the business was to be sold. How would that benefit her?" Miss P tapped a file in front of her.

"Only if the business is worth a lot of money." Sam lifted her gaze from her computer. "Which it's not. It's providing a good living, but ..." Sam shrugged.

Zoe raised her hand.

"You can speak out, Zoe."

"I wasn't sure." She flashed them a grin. "Maybe she didn't care about the business. Maybe all she wanted was out from under it. I know I would."

"Zoe might be right." Mac gazed at her former classmate. "She brings up a good point too. We've been stuck on one way of looking at this. It's time to change our perspective. What other reasons could there be to want Doug dead besides money?"

"Love, money, and power are the big three." Sam held up as many fingers.

"What about fear?" Zoe asked.

"Fear of what?" Mac rose and walked to the refrigerator.

"I don't know. Maybe fear of having your past exposed."

Mac turned and wrinkled her brow at Zoe. What did she mean by that? Was she referring to their earlier conversation concerning the work she was doing with Nate? But Zoe wasn't paying any attention to her.

"Fear of someone discovering your secret." Zoe continued.

"What secret could Laura have that she'd be afraid would be discovered?" Sam asked.

Mac poured herself a glass of iced tea. "I could think of a few, but I'd be speculating." She returned to the table.

"Like what?" Sam asked.

"She was still married when she married Doug. Laura whatever wasn't her real name. She had an illegitimate child. She'd been in prison." Mac took a drink.

"Wow." Zoe gave her a wide-eyed look. "You're a little spooky."

"That's Mac." Sam laughed. "Her mind works in mysterious ways."

"The assumption is that Douglas was divorcing her because he'd discovered her secret." Miss P removed her glasses. "She killed him to keep the reason for the divorce from coming to light." She polished the lenses and replaced them on her nose. "This will require more research."

"I know." Mac's gaze bounced from Miss P to Sam. "I'm leaving that to you two. But I'll also make a call to Beth, my oldest sister, to see if she knows anything about Laura."

"We've talked about money as a motive and fear, but what about love?" Miss P peered at them over her glasses.

"Love?" Zoe raised her eyebrows. "How would that fit?"

"My dear, many men and women are driven to kill by frustrated desire. If he or she can't have their beloved, no one can."

Sam absently stroked her belly. "Do you think she would have killed him because he wanted to divorce her?"

"She doesn't strike me as the type." Visions of Laura kissing Jake made Mac's stomach churn. "More like the predatory type."

"I believe you're correct." Miss P pushed to her feet.

"Who's correct about what?" Jake appeared in the kitchen doorway.

Motives and murder forgotten, Mac hurried to his side. "Laura James was more predatory than a woman filled with frustrated desire for her husband."

"You got that right." He pulled her close.

Mac's phone rang and Jake released her. "Chief Baker." Her gaze swept the room, and she pressed the speaker button. "Any news?"

"We're holding Mrs. Green until we get the results back on her revolver."

A heavy sigh escaped her lips.

"I know it's not what you want, but that's the way it is." His tone brooked no argument. "We can't rule her out until the evidence proves her innocent."

"Thanks for letting us know."

"Another thing." His voice softened a little. "Zachary Zane's been spotted out by the fairgrounds."

"I'd like to be there when you talk to him." Mac hand tightened on the phone.

"I'll think about it. I need to speak to Jake. Privately."

Mac took the phone off speaker and handed it to Jake. If he stayed close, she should be able to overhear their conversation. But he turned his back to her and went into the foyer. She ground her teeth and waited. A moment later, he returned.

"What was that all about?" Mac eyed him.

"The Chief needs me back." Jake handed her the phone. "At least part-time. When do you think Alan will get home?"

Sam glanced at the clock. "I don't think he has any evening clients, so probably in about two hours. For dinner."

"Good." Jake snagged a soft drink from the fridge. "What else have you ladies been talking about?"

"Possible motives for Laura James to kill her husband." Miss P arranged some cheese and crackers on a plate and set it on the table. "We discussed money, fear, and love, but didn't find one that seemed to suit."

"So all speculation." Jake took a drink.

"Yes."

"But you still think it was Laura who arranged with Zane to switch the fuses."

"Yes." Mac took her empty glass to the sink. "I guess we'll have to see what Zane has to say. When they finally catch him."

"They've got him." Jake finished his drink and threw the can in the garbage.

# CHAPTER 30

The fatigue dropped away as a newfound energy seized Jake's body. The Chief needed him. He was going back to work, doing what he was good at.

Mac rounded on him. "How do you know they've got Zane?"

"The Chief told me. That's part of the reason he wants me back. To interview him."

Mac slammed her glass so hard it bounced off the counter. Jake caught it before it hit the floor, and their eyes locked.

"I've been working so hard on this," Mac whispered. "It's rough to be shut out when it's all coming together."

"I've already got permission for you to watch the interview," Jake said quietly.

"You can wipe that silly grin off your face any time." Mac pointed her finger at him. "I'm beginning to think you love your work more than me."

"Two different things." His grin broadened. "Entirely."

She pulled into the parking spot with Jake's name on it and

turned off the car. "Thanks for arranging for me to watch the interview."

"I need a driver, and the Chief deputized you." He struggled to unlock his belt. He'd be glad when he had the use of both his hands again. "It wasn't hard."

"Let me get that." She leaned closer.

He tilted her face to meet his. "I love you, Mackenzie, more than life itself."

"I know." She kissed him. "I was only kidding."

Sometimes she was kidding, but other times he knew she needed to be reassured. He had those times too. Probably everyone did.

The sight of the familiar building warmed him, and he couldn't wait to get inside. He grabbed Mac by the hand and pulled her along the sidewalk.

"Jake, good to see you back." The woman behind the reception desk gave him a warm smile. "Hi, Mackenzie. I'll let the Chief know you're here."

"You're a sight for sore eyes." Chief Baker came at Jake with both arms open wide to give him a big bear hug, but stopped and eyed the sling on his left arm. "I guess that will have to wait."

"Yes, sir." Jake grinned at him. He had a feeling he'd be doing a lot of grinning for a while. "But I can shake hands."

The Chief pumped his hand with vigor. "Okay. Down to business." The older man waved a hand in front of him. "You're going to have to wipe that smirk off your face."

"Yes, sir." He dredged his stony detective face from storage and put it on.

"We've got Zane in Room Two." Chief Baker looked back at Mac. "You can watch on a monitor in Jake's office." He nodded to an officer who led her away. "I pulled Young in to do the interview with you."

"Vic? I heard he was back at work. How are the other officers?"

"A little banged up, but patrolling the streets again. They've got a story to tell their children."

"Not the kind of story I'd wish on them." Jake ran a hand through his hair. Vic limped toward him. "Good to see you, buddy."

"You too." The slim man shook Jake's hand. "You saved my life."

"From the looks of it, I gave you a gimp leg."

"A piece of shrapnel. Nothing serious. It's healing." Vic inclined his head toward Jake's bandage. "Nothing like a broken shoulder."

"That's life. Right?" Jake shrugged his unbroken one. "I hear we're interviewing Zane together."

"Looking forward to it."

"Let's go."

Zane sat in the same white plastic chair where so many others had sat before. Jake sat next to the desk in the back of the room, and Vic Young took a seat directly across from Zane.

"State your name and address for the record." Vic folded his hands on his lap.

"Zachary Zane. I used to live at my sister's place, but ..." The man placed his head in his hands and bent over.

Jake glanced at Vic. They gave Zane a moment to compose himself.

"Mr. Zane, do you know why you're here?" Vic asked.

He nodded.

"You'll have to answer yes or no."

"Yes." Zane's Adam's apple bobbed convulsively. "You think I tried to kill Mr. James."

"Did you?"

"No." He raised a dirty face streaked with the tracks of his tears. "I only did what I was told."

"And what were you told?" Jake rolled closer to him.

"To let someone have my key to the room where the fuse panel is." Zane turned pleading eyes on Jake. "I didn't know what was going to happen."

"Who told you to give your key away?"

"Mrs. White."

Jake resisted the urge to look at the camera in the corner of the room where he knew Mac was watching. "Mrs. White told you to give your key to someone?"

"Yes." Zane lifted his shoulders a little. "Well, not Mrs. White herself."

"Then who?" This was the point in a case that Jake lived for. The point when everything came together. The point when all the hard work paid off.

Jake knew the answer to his question already. Laura James. All he needed was confirmation, and then he could get on with the next part. To find out who killed Laura. He leaned forward.

"Ms. Underwood came to me and told me Mrs. White said I was to give her my key for her brother so he could let the electrician in."

# CHAPTER 31

"Not Laura James?" Jake blurted the words before he could stop himself.

"No, sir." Zane shook his head. "She doesn't look anything like Ms. Underwood. No way I'd get them two mixed up."

"When did Francis Underwood borrow the key?" Vic asked.

Zane kneaded his brow in thought. "Two days before Mr. James's accident?"

Jake stood and turned to Vic. "We need to talk."

In the hall, Jake led the way to the Chief's office. "Something's come up."

"Sit." The Chief pointed to two chairs in front of his desk.

"We came into this interview ninety percent sure Laura James was the one who asked Zane to switch the fuses." Jake inclined his head at Vic. "But he just told us that Francis Underwood asked him for the key to the electrical closet for her brother."

"So, now you think Thomas Underwood messed with the fuses?"

"Could be."

"What about the sister?"

Jake looked at Vic. "An unwitting accomplice? She's a nurse, and she was pretty broke up about his accident."

"At this point, I'd say focus on Thomas." Vic nodded.

"Time we had a chat with Mr. Underwood." The Chief leaned back in his chair.

"I'll send a couple of officers to get him." Vic rose and left the room.

"So you don't think Zane was involved?" Chief Baker drilled his gaze into Jake.

"No." Jake met his stare.

"Why'd he run?"

"He has a record, and he knew he'd been set up to take the fall. I'll ask him." Jake rubbed his bandaged arm. "It could have worked if Zane had been blown up in the blast along with his sister. We might have put it down to suicide."

"Maybe." Chief Baker opened a file on his desk. "Is there anything you can charge him with? Keep him in custody for a few days?"

"Withholding information. Hampering an investigation." Jake stood. "That should be enough."

"Good. We should know more by then."

And Zane would be safe. Jake returned to the interview room. The wiry little man lifted aquamarine eyes filled with despair.

"If you had nothing to do with Mr. James's accident, why'd you run?" Jake searched the man's face for any shadow of dishonesty, but saw none.

"I have not always been a good man." He pointed at the file in Jake's hand. "I'm sure you already know this. When Mr. James was hurt, and you found out the fuses had been switched, I knew someone was trying to make it look like I did this." He tapped his chest. "Like I was being bad again."

"Who do you think this someone is?"

Zane shook his head.

"You're safe here. We're charging you with a couple of small things and keeping you here for a couple of days."

"But what about after?"

He had a point. Jake rose. "The officer will read you your rights and the charges. We'll talk again tomorrow." At the door, Jake turned. "Do you have any idea who was behind the bombing at your sister's house?"

"No." Zane's eyes darkened. "But my sweet sister didn't deserve to die. Find the monster, Detective Sanders."

"I'll do my best." Jake held his gaze a moment longer. "But it would help if you told me who you think tried to frame you." Jake left the room and went back to his office.

The grim look on Mac's face told him she'd heard everything. "We had it all wrong."

She was right, but he didn't have the energy to hash it out right then. "I'm tired." He took her arm. "Let's go."


MAC DROVE BACK to Sam's on autopilot, her mind working to undo all the false assumptions about Laura James and come up with new ones for Thomas Underwood. She looked forward to brainstorming with Sam and Miss P and Zoe.

Light snoring came from the passenger seat, where Jake slumped against the door. Hopefully, Alan was home to help get her fiancé to bed. His time at the police station had wiped him out.

When the car stopped, Jake sat up and yawned. "Sorry. Guess I'm more tired than I realized."

"Wait here. I'll see if Alan's home."

"I don't need help." He swung his feet out and stood—for a

second. Then one foot got tangled and he buckled, whacking his injured arm on the door on the way down. He ended up seated in the car once more. "I guess I could use some help."

Mac hurried to the house. "Alan, can you help Jake?"

"Coming." He pulled his coat on. "Hope he didn't damage his shoulder."

Mac swallowed the words she'd been about to say about the stubbornness of men. "Thanks." She could be pretty hardheaded too. "I'll wait here." She opened the door for them and beeped her car locked.

"Here." Jake handed her purse to her. "It's not my color anyway."

She chuckled and kissed him. "I love you."

"Love you more," he whispered against her lips. "I'm going to bed. See you tomorrow. Figure this out, okay?"

"I'll try." She kissed him again. "Sweet dreams."

"Come on, buddy, I'll help you get ready for bed." Alan put a hand on Jake's good shoulder. "I want to take a look at your stitches."

Mac hung her coat on the rack and headed for the kitchen. It was so quiet. She scanned the attached family room. Sam reclined among a nest of blankets, her eyes closed. There was no sign of the others. She leaned against the counter and released a stream of air from puffed cheeks. This wasn't what she'd envisioned.

Alan came in and poured water into the coffee machine.

"Where are Miss P and Zoe?" Mac asked.

"They left about twenty minutes ago. Miss P said they were going back to her house."

Mac nodded. Zoe was going over to work with Nate. She looked at her phone. "Did they say if they were coming back?"

"I don't know." Alan inclined his head toward the family room. "You'd have to ask Sam."

Or call Miss P. Mac punched her number. "Hi, Miss P. I just got back to Sam's."

"I'm about ready to leave here. Why don't I meet you at your house?"

"You don't have to do that. I'll be fine." Mac rubbed the back of her neck. "Isn't it a little late for Zoe and Nate to be working?"

"She tired of sitting around and asked if I'd bring her over here so she could make better use of her time. I gave her permission to stay the night." The older woman's voice held a note of indecision that Mac hadn't heard before. "After all, they are both grown adults."

"Why don't you stay home tonight? I'll see if I can spend the night here at Sam's."

"Are you sure?" The relief in her voice was unmistakable.

"I'm sure. I'll see you here in the morning. And bring Zoe." Mac paused. "We need to go back to the beginning. Again." Their powwow would have to wait until tomorrow.

"I overheard what you said about staying here." Alan gave her a smile. "And the answer is, of course. We haven't started making the third bedroom into a nursery yet."

"Don't you think you'd better get started on the conversion?" Mac raised her eyebrows at him.

"Yep." He gazed across the room at his contented wife. "We have a bassinet for our bedroom, and I sometimes wonder if she isn't secretly planning on keeping Elizabeth in with us until she goes to college."

"I don't think you have to worry about that." Mac chuckled. "She'll change her mind pretty quick after your baby's here and neither of you is getting any sleep."

"Thanks for the encouragement." He furrowed his brow. "I think." He led her down the hall to a small bedroom with a twin bed. "You'll have to make it up yourself. Sorry. I need to take care of Samantha. Night, Mac."

"Night, Alan. Thanks." Mac fitted the bottom sheet, tucked in the top sheet, and replaced the quilt on the bed. A soft knock sounded at the door.

"Mac?" Sam's voice sounded on the other side.

"You should be in bed by now." Mac hugged her friend.

"I thought you might want one of Alan's clean T-shirts to sleep in." Sam smiled at her. "I'm glad you're here with us tonight. I'll sleep better."

"Yeah. Me too." Mac closed the door and laid the T-shirt on the bed. She tossed her phone on the quilt next to it.

The cozy room would make a great nursery. She closed the curtains on the large, south-facing window. Plenty of light. That was good. A rocker would fit perfectly in the far corner. She could picture Sam with baby Elizabeth—

Her phone rang and vibrated on top of the bed.

"Somebody's trying to get in." Zoe's low tone carried a note of panic.

# CHAPTER 32

Mac pressed a clammy palm to her forehead. "Get off the phone with me and call nine-one-one. Now. I'm on my way." If anything happened to Zoe or Miss P, she'd never forgive herself.

"But—"

Mac didn't wait to hear what Zoe had to say. She hung up and raced out of the room. "Sam." She burst into Sam and Alan's bedroom. "Somebody is after Zoe and Nate. I'm leaving."

"Do you need a gun?"

Did she? Mac hated carrying her gun, but ... "Give it to me."

"What's all the commotion?" Jake poked his head into the hall.

"Zoe and Nate are in danger." Mac tucked the gun into her waistband.

"Wait. I'll go with you."

Mac hesitated. How could she tell him she didn't think he was ready? He was the love of her life. Her man. How could she hurt him like that? But she was wasting time.

"No." Alan faced off with Jake. "You are not ready for active duty. As your therapist, I will not allow you to go. You will endanger yourself and Mac." He turned to Mac. "Go."

She threw Jake a look of love mixed with sorrow and ran out the door. In the car, she called the station house to make sure Zoe had reported the intruder.

When Mac arrived, two officers manned the gates into the courtyard, where several patrol cars strobed red, blue, and white lights against Miss P's house. Mac pulled into a space and got out.

She cast an eye over the crowd gathered outside the gates before heading for the house. Was that Francis Underwood? Shadows made it difficult to tell for sure. What would she be doing here?

Miss P opened the door for her. "I'm glad you're here."

"What happened?" Mac followed her friend to the front parlor. Like most homes on rivers or lakes, the side facing the water is considered the front. Mac entered through the back door.

"I will let Zoe tell you."

Zoe nestled on a large pillow by the fire with a throw around her shoulders. Nate sat close by.

"Tell me. I'm listening." Mac sat on the floor in front of Zoe.

"We'd finished for the evening." Zoe inclined her head at Nate. "Nate went to bed. Miss P was already in bed." She swallowed. "I turned out the lights except the ones over the sink and in the hall. I was going to take a snack to my room." She cut her eyes to the doorway. "Miss P said it was okay."

"Go on." Mac nodded at her.

"I bent down to get some chips out of the cupboard, and that's when I heard it. Somebody tried the door handle." Zoe put a shaky hand to her mouth. "I stayed low and crab-walked into the hallway."

"That's when you called me."

Zoe nodded.

"Then what?"

"You hung up on me." Zoe glared at her.

"I told you to call nine-one-one." Mac met her stare. "And that I was on my way."

"I did. But whoever was out there broke the glass in the door and reached through to unlock it. I wasn't going to wait for him to get in, so I grabbed a knife and stabbed his hand." Zoe made a thrust with her empty fist.

"What were you thinking?" A shiver of what could have been ran through Mac. "You could have been killed. What if he'd shot through the door?"

"What was I supposed to do? Let them come in? Hurt Miss P? Nate? Me? I didn't know how long it would take for the police or you to get here." Tears streamed down her face. "And you told me not to use my gun unless absolutely necessary. Remember?"

"I'm sorry." Mac hugged her. "You're right. I ... the thought of you and Miss P and Nate being in danger while working on my parents' case is too much for me." She shook her head. "I think—"

"No. Do not say it." Zoe pointed a finger at her. "Do not tell us to stop investigating this case." Her eyes grew hard. "This is personal now. Those dirtbags aren't going to get to me." She turned to look at Nate.

"I agree." He looked at Miss P. "Can we up the security on the property?"

"Certainly."

Mac stared into the fire. "Why would they risk breaking into a house where they know there are at least two people?"

"We've been discussing this." Miss P perched on a chair. "We believe they were after the files."

"Have you found something?" Mac focused her gaze on Nate.

"I think so." He left the room. In a moment, he was back, a thick folder in his hands. "From what I can tell," Nate lowered his voice and glanced around to make sure none of the forensics or police officers were nearby, "your parents found out that Quinton Underwood was embezzling money from their business."

"Underwood. I should have known." Mac clenched her fists. "It looks like his son, Thomas, may have been behind Doug's electrocution."

"I thought Laura—" Zoe threw her a perplexed look.

"Things have changed. I'd hoped to hash it out with you and Miss P and Sam tonight, but it can wait." Mac waved a hand at Nate. "Go on."

"Your parents couldn't get involved in a messy lawsuit that might make the papers. So, they did something very clever." Nate tapped the file. "They investigated other firms that Underwood worked for and found out he was skimming money from Fischer Industries as well. Which, as you know, does work for the government."

"Which makes his appropriation of funds a federal crime." The words burst from Mac's mouth in astonishment. "Quinton Underwood killed my parents."

"Mac, we don't know that for a fact, but it seems most likely. Especially since we discovered that your parents and Oliver DeLuca seem to have settled their differences out of court and DeLuca went back to Italy."

"What happened to Quinton Underwood?"

"He served time in a federal prison for embezzling." Nate locked eyes with her. "He was released a month ago."

The air in the room seemed to drop ten degrees, and Mac moved closer to the fire. "Where is he?"

"We don't know for sure, but the last we heard, he was living somewhere near Dutzow."

"That's close. Why would he move back here?"

Nate shrugged. "To be close to his son and daughter? Who knows."

"Or to make sure I don't find the evidence to prove he killed my parents." Mac stood and paced the room. "Zoe, was the hand you stabbed wearing a glove?"

"Yeah. A black leather one."

"The police have the knife?" Mac stopped in front of her. She nodded.

"Good." Mac pulled her phone out and dialed the Chief's number. She went into the kitchen. The area by the door had crime scene tape around it, and the forensics team worked inside the tape carefully gathering all the evidence. Glass covered the floor and blood spattered parts of the door.

"Chief Baker."

"I'm sorry to call so late, but I need your help." Mac told the Chief what happened and asked that the blood on the knife and the door be checked against Quinton Underwood.

"I'll make sure of it." His tone was determined. "You know I was there. With your sister, Beth. I want to get this guy as much as you do."

"I know." Mac's throat closed and she couldn't say more. She pressed End.

# CHAPTER 33

Awet tongue on the cheek launched Mac out of bed, sending Killer scurrying for cover. She dried her face with the sheet. "It's okay, boy. You can come in." She must not have latched her door all the way.

The goldendoodle bounced over to her, sat, and offered his paw.

"You are the sweetest dog in the whole world." Mac drew him in for a hug and ran a hand down his soft fur. "Who's making breakfast? It smells yummy." She pulled on her jeans. "Go on. I'll be there in a minute."

Alan presided over eggs, bacon, and toast while Sam sat at the table in front of her computer.

"You made it in time for one of my home-cooked meals." Alan set a plate by Sam. "Five more minutes, and I'd be gone."

"Whew. That was close." Mac pulled out a chair at the end of the table. "What are you doing?" She leaned toward Sam.

"I talked to Miss P this morning." She moved the mouse around and clicked. "She told me what happened last night and about Quinton Underwood. I thought I'd start looking into him."

"Find anything interesting?"

"Not beyond what we already know." Sam squinted at the screen. "But I'm just getting started."

"When they get here, I want to revisit Doug's case from the beginning." Mac inhaled the aromas from her plate. "Thanks, Alan. You're the best."

"Better than me?" Jake kissed her on the top of the head.

"I refuse to answer on the grounds it may incriminate me."

"Oh man." Jake splayed a hand across his chest. "I'm crushed."

Alan sighed. "One more breakfast plate coming up. And then I really do have to leave."

"I can do it." Jake walked over to the stove.

"No way." Alan blocked him. "Nobody uses my stove. Especially a man with only one good arm."

Jake threw up his hand. "Just offering."

"You sit and help these two solve their cases." Alan slid two eggs onto a plate along with four slices of bacon. "Toast in a minute."

The doorbell rang.

"I'll get it." Mac pushed her chair back and hurried down the hall. Miss P and Zoe stood on the front porch. "Come in."

"What smells so good?" Zoe took a deep breath.

"Alan cooked us breakfast."

The two women shed their coats and followed Mac back to the kitchen.

"You got any left?" Zoe made a beeline for the stove and Alan.

He peered at her. "Didn't you have breakfast before you came?"

"Yes, but that was an hour ago."

"Sit." He gestured with his spatula.

She pecked him on the cheek.

He glared at her.

Mac gathered Sam's plate along with hers and Jake's, and took them to the sink. "We have work to do. It seems Laura wasn't the one who got Zane to switch the fuses like we thought."

"Who did?" Zoe paused between bites.

"Francis Underwood told Zane that Mrs. White wanted him to give his key to Francis for her brother, Thomas."

"That Thomas needed it for the electrician." Jake shifted in his chair.

"Did Mrs. White tell Francis to get the key for Thomas?" Miss P asked.

"We haven't asked her yet, but I doubt it." Mac shook her head. "I think she would have said something in the beginning."

"So now we turn our attention to Thomas Underwood." The older woman sat back and folded her hands in her lap.

"Yes," Mac said. "Let's go back to our motives—love, money, fear, and power. Which would work for Thomas?"

Zoe wiped her mouth on a napkin. "If he loved Laura, I guess he could have wanted Doug out of the way."

"But then why would he protest stopping the machines?" Sam looked up from her computer.

"Maybe he panicked and realized that if Doug died, it would be murder, and not attempted murder?" Mac made a note on her pad.

"That is possible," Miss P said. "Or he realized Laura didn't love him and he'd almost killed a man for nothing."

"But can you see him setting a bomb in Zane's sister's

house? He knew that would end in murder." Mac glanced at her list of motives. "What about money? As a limited partner in Doug's business, Thomas was due to inherit a large chunk of money and have first refusal to buy the company from Laura."

"However, Douglas's will stated that the company was to be sold upon his death." Miss P peered at them over her glasses.

"But I don't think Thomas knew about the stipulation until after the electrocution." Mac tapped her pencil on her tablet. "Which is why he fought with Laura about turning off the machines."

"Except the company isn't worth much," Sam said. "I think Thomas could have bought it back with no problem."

"Unless ..." The shadow of an idea flitted around the edges of Mac's mind.

"Unless what?" Jake asked.

"Unless like father, like son." Mac held up her hands. "Listen. What if Underwood arranged to electrocute Doug, thinking that he would end up with the company?"

"We've already been through this." Sam tilted her head at Mac. "Laura got half."

"He had first rights of refusal if she wanted to sell it. Or maybe that didn't bother him. Maybe he didn't care if he owned the whole company. He'd still have control over the money." Mac rolled her hand in a circle. "Then somehow he discovers that Doug's will states that the company must be sold. Which wouldn't be too bad either. He could always buy it back. Except for one thing."

"What?" Sam threw up her hands. "Get to the point."

"The sale would require an audit." Mac gave them a sly grin. "And then he would be in deep trouble. He's been skimming from the company for years." She lifted her shoulders. "I don't know that for sure, but it's a theory."

"But if Underwood is making a good living off Doug's company, why try to kill him?" Jake asked.

The answer came to Mac in a flash. "Because Doug found out."

# CHAPTER 34

Mac took a drink of her water. If her theory was correct, and Doug did discover Underwood had been embezzling money from his company, then Thomas Underwood could be the person behind his accident, thinking that would solve his problem. He knew about Doug's atrial fibrillation too.

The irony was that if he'd been successful in killing Doug, the company would have been put up for sale, and his crime would have come to light anyway. What a stroke of luck for Thomas Underwood that Doug ended up in a coma. No wonder he was so adamant about leaving his friend on life support. It gave him a chance to plan a way out of his predicament. Did he kill Laura too?

"I need to call the Chief." Jake pulled his phone from his pocket and left the room.

Jake didn't know why they hadn't seen it to begin with. It made perfect sense. He rubbed the back of his neck. But when someone was attacked, the first suspect was the spouse. Granted, Zane pointed them to Thomas Underwood, but Mac clarified the motive for him.

Once they had him in custody, it shouldn't be any trouble getting the truth out of him. There were still loose ends. The bombing, for instance, and the whereabouts of the gun that killed Laura James. But those should be cleared up when they talked to him.

"We still haven't found him." The Chief growled over the line. "When we do, I want you here."

"Good. I want to be there." Jake glanced over his shoulder. "Mac will—"

"She can come watch."

"Thanks." Life would be a lot easier for him. "Let me know."

"By the way, tell Mac the blood is a match. I sent it for DNA testing."

"What blood?" Unease settled like a rock in the pit of his stomach.

"Ask her."

He intended to do just that. He pocketed his phone and strode back to the kitchen, where she waited gnawing on a thumbnail.

"Have they got him?" She placed her hands on his chest and turned her face up to his.

"Not yet." He couldn't help but raise his hand to her cheek. "The Chief asked me to tell you the blood was a match and that he's sent it for DNA testing." He furrowed his brow at her. "What blood?"

"From last night at Miss P's house. The intruder." She dropped her hands and returned to her seat at the table. "We think it may have been Quinton Underwood, Thomas's father. He worked for my mom and dad." She motioned for him to sit. "Nate found evidence that points to him as my parents' killer, and he may be trying to stop my investigation into their death."

"Why didn't he try to destroy the evidence long ago?"

"He was in prison. It's a long story."

Jake raised a hand. "You can tell me later when we have more time." He glanced at the clock. "I need a shower. We need to be ready to leave for the station when they bring *Thomas* Underwood in for questioning."

"We?" Her eyes widened.

"The Chief agreed to let you listen in again." He stood.

Mac jumped up and threw her arms around his neck. "Thanks, sweetheart."

"You're right. We make a good team." He buried his face in her hair and prayed he wouldn't regret those words. "Be back in ten."

It took him longer than he thought. Everything did these days. He couldn't wait to get the use of both his arms again. Getting dressed was the hardest, but he finally finished and got back to the kitchen. "Any news?

"No." Mac looked up from her notes. "What do you think about me dropping you at the station and taking Miss P to our office?" she stretched. "You could get caught up on what's been going on and Miss P and I could get some work done. Zoe can stay here with Sam. I'll leave my car for her in case we need her."

"Where will you be?"

"I'll be at the office until you need me, then I'll join you at the police station."

He'd rather wait at the station than here. That was for sure. And he could use the time to get acclimated again. "Sounds good." He grabbed his coat. "You sure you know how to drive Miss P's boat?"

Mac gave him an are-you-for-real look. "Get in the car, Sanders."

"So now it's Sanders. What happened to sweetheart?" He plopped into the backseat.

"You two remind me of my students." Miss P slid onto the passenger seat. "Always teasing each other."

Not always. He caught Mac's gaze in the rearview mirror. He remembered how she felt in his arms, the pressure of her lips on his, the taste of her skin.

"Mackenzie, please pay attention to the road." Miss P's sharp tone filled the car.

He grinned and looked away. At the station parking lot, he leaned forward. "I'll call when Thomas Underwood is in custody." He touched Mac's shoulder. "Be careful."

"Always." Mac blew him a kiss.

Jake stood inside the glass doors and watched the large sedan drive away. Although the day was sunny, clouds of unease cast shadows on his mind. He'd feel a lot better when the Underwoods, father and son, were both in custody.

"You going up?" Vic clapped him on his good shoulder.

"Yeah." Jake turned and started up the stairs to the precinct on the second floor.

"You're here." The Chief lifted his eyebrows at him.

"I got tired of waiting at home." Jake inclined his head down the hall. "Thought I'd catch up on some paperwork."

"Fine. Always good to have you around."

Jake hung his coat on the rack and walked around his desk to his chair. The one he'd been sitting in for years. It fit him, and he let out a sigh of recognition as he sat. He was back at work.

After sorting through the files in his inbox, he chose one to focus on. It was something he could finish and check off his list with little effort.

Ten minutes later, Vic popped his head in the door. "We've got Thomas Underwood. They're bringing him in for questioning now."

Adrenaline surged through his body. Like a fighter before a fight, or an athlete before an important meet. At least that's how he always imagined it. He dialed Mac's number.

A recorded voice came on. "I'm sorry. The number you have dialed is not available. If you'd like to leave a message—"

He must have pressed the wrong button. Same response. The clouds of unease in Jake's mind darkened.

# CHAPTER 35

Mac glanced in the rearview mirror as she drove away from the police station. Jake had given her that smile again. The one that made her stomach flip. Would it be that way the rest of their lives? She hoped so.

"Mackenzie, we need to take a left here, my dear." Miss P's voice broke through her reverie.

"Sorry." Heat climbed her cheeks. "My mind was on something else."

"Or someone else, perhaps."

Mac slowed to turn into the driveway. Maneuvering Miss P's big sedan was very different from her smaller one, and she didn't want to scrape the fender. "We're here. All in one piece."

"I expected nothing less." Miss P swung out of the car and shut the door.

Maybe she didn't, but Mac wasn't too sure. She got out and locked the car before following Miss P up the sidewalk to the porch.

"Oh dear." Miss P's distraught voice carried back to Mac.

"What is it?" Mac hopped onto the porch and inched the

older woman to one side. "You've got to be kidding." The interior of the office looked like a group of cowboys had a drunken brawl in there. Not one surface or piece of furniture was left untouched. This wasn't the first time this had happened. "I'll call nine-one-one."

"I don't think so." A man came out of the shadows and pressed a gun to her side. "Phone, please." He shoved them over the threshold into the office and slammed the door. "Now I'll take your phone as well, Miss Freebody."

"I'm expecting a call from the police any moment." Mac tried to catch a glimpse of the man, but couldn't. "When I don't answer, they'll come looking for me."

"We won't be here long. I want the files. You know which ones." He increased the pressure of his pistol barrel on her ribs. "Don't waste time."

"They are at my house." Miss P looked over her shoulder at the man. "Quinton Underwood. You've aged rather badly."

"That's what prison does to you." He hissed at them.

"You know, we weren't sure if you killed the Loves or if Oliver DeLuca had." Miss P turned. "But now we know for certain."

"Don't give me that. You could tell from the lawyer's files." He eyed her.

"Not really." She folded her hands in front of her.

The force of the gun against Mac's side lessened as Underwood listened to Miss P. Mac eased herself forward a half-step.

"I have copies here if you'd like to see them." Miss P waved an elegant hand over the mess.

Underwood shook his head. "I looked everywhere. There are no documents here that go back that far."

"We have a hidden safe."

He narrowed his eyes at her. "Show me." He waved the gun in Mac's face. "If you try anything, I will shoot her."

Miss P paled. "I understand." She led them into Mac's office, where the safe lay hidden under the floor.

Once inside, Miss P stumbled and fell into Underwood. His attention diverted, Mac grabbed his gun hand and bit down hard. She steeled herself against the crunch of tissue and bone.

The big man roared and threw his arm out as if to toss her aside like a dog.

But she held on, pushing her teeth deeper into his flesh. His heavy gun hit the floor with a thunk. He crooked his arm and yanked her back to his chest.

His black eyes met hers. "You are a dead woman." He grabbed her hair with his left hand and wrenched it back.

Mac screamed as he flung her across the room.

A shot rang out.

Quinton Underwood jerked. As if in slow motion, he turned to face the older woman holding his gun.

"That one was for my friend, Mackenzie's mother, and this one"—another shot echoed in the room—"is for her father."

Underwood fell to his knees before crashing to the floor. The old wood transmitted the reverberation through the soles of Mac's shoes.

JAKE HURRIED into the hallway and grabbed Vic's arm. "I need you to drive me to Mac's office."

"But what about Thomas Underwood?" Vic raised his chin toward the interview room.

"He'll have to wait. I think Mac's in trouble." Jake took the stairs as fast as he dared. Apprehension filled him with urgency. He had to get to Mac.

"What gives?" Vic jumped behind the wheel and started the SUV.

"I know something's wrong." He held up a hand to silence objections. "I can't explain it."

"No explanation needed." Vic hit the lights and siren. "Call for another unit to meet us there."

Jake made the call and tried to focus on praying for safety for Mac and Miss P. They rounded the corner onto Second Street. Everything looked normal. Light from Mac's office shone onto the yard. The big sedan sat in the driveway.

Had he dragged Vic over here for nothing? Had he been away from the job too long? Lost his touch? His instinct? The SUV pulled to the curb and Jake leaped out.

"Wait." Vic ran to catch up with him. "We don't know what we're walking into. We should wait for back-up."

Jake shook his head. He drew his weapon and marched up the lawn and onto the porch. Vic followed, gun drawn and down in front of him. At the front door, Vic held up three fingers and pointed to himself. Jake nodded. Vic tried the nob. He gave Jake a thumbs-up.

"Police," Vic yelled before shoving the door open. He swept the room with his gun. "What a mess," he murmured.

Jake stepped in behind him. His throat tightened at the devastation before his eyes. "Mac, Miss P." His words rose in a wail of agony.

"We're in here."

He brought his gun up and moved quickly across to the doorway into Mac's private office.

"We're okay."

Jake lowered his gun and stepped inside. He took in the scene in astonished silence. The acrid smell of gunpowder mixed with the metallic odor of fresh blood filled the air. Miss

P stood immediately in front of Jake, her back to him, ramrod straight, and a pistol in her right hand.

A big man sprawled face down on the floor six feet from her, his arms extended on either side. One hand wounded with what looked like a bite mark. Mackenzie leaned against a table across the room. Her eyes seemed huge in a pale face, and her mouth and chin were covered in blood.

"Are you …" He didn't know what to ask. Part of him wanted to shout for joy that Mac was alive, and part of him wanted to scream because he wasn't here to save her.

"I'll be better when I can clean up." She raised a hand to her mouth. "Get forensics. Please."

"I've called them." Vic approached Miss P. "It's over now." He gently put a hand on her shoulder. "I need the gun." He moved his hand to where she gripped the pistol. "Let me have the gun, Miss P."

She released it. "He killed my friends."

"This is Quinton Underwood?" Vic asked.

She sighed and folded her hands in front of her. "Yes."

"What was he after?" He dropped the gun into a bag.

"Quinton knew Mackenzie was looking into her parents' death." Miss P gazed at Mac. "He hoped to destroy the files from their lawyer, and anything that would incriminate him." She shook her head. "You saw the mess he made of our beautiful office. We must have arrived shortly after he finished, and he decided to go a step further. I'm certain that after he gained the documents, he would have killed Mackenzie and me."

"How did you get his gun off him?"

"Ingenuity and teamwork." A grim smile played across Miss P's lips. "Never underestimate a determined woman, detective."

Jake listened to the conversation between Miss P and Vic,

but kept his focus on Mac. Staying close to the walls, Jake circled the room. "The crime scene investigators should be here soon." He reached his hand toward the dried blood on the back of her head. "Did he hit you?"

"No. He yanked me by the hair. I think some of my scalp is gone." Mac touched the spot and gave a sharp intake of breath. "I hope it grows back."

Anger clouded his vision and short-circuited his hearing. Someone tapped him on the shoulder.

"Detective, let me through, please." An evidence analyst pushed past him.

He stepped back against the wall. Several men and women moved around the room, taking photos and measurements. Their movements were quick and efficient. One swabbed Miss P's hands and led her away to change into a white jumpsuit. He felt about as useful as a screen door on a submarine.

"Miss Love needs to go to the hospital to get her wound treated." The analyst placed a swab in her kit. "But first, I'll help her change."

Jake nodded. "What can I do?"

"Get an ambulance."

That he could do. He retraced his steps to the doorway and out into the reception area, where more technicians worked collecting evidence. A commotion on the porch caught his attention.

"I need to see him." A frantic female voice rang out above the sounds in the house. "He's my father."

Jake hurried outside to where Vic and an officer blocked entry to Francis Underwood.

# CHAPTER 36

"What are you doing here?" Jake faced off with Francis Underwood.

"I heard shots." She pointed toward the house. "I wanted to make sure my father is okay."

"That's not what I asked." He narrowed his gaze.

As the real meaning of Jake's question sank in, a shadow climbed her neck and suffused her cheeks. "I ... I've been following my father."

"Why?"

Francis seemed to shrink before him. "I was afraid he would do something rash."

"Like what?" The tone of his voice lowered with each question.

"Did he hurt Mackenzie or Miss P?"

Her words were so soft he almost couldn't hear them.

He stared at Francis for a long moment. She'd known her father was dangerous and done nothing. Mac and Miss P could have been killed. His hands curled into fists.

But the women were alive. He stuffed his emotions behind

his professional persona once more. "They'll live." He sighed and relaxed his hands. "However, I'm sorry to inform you that your father is dead."

A keening wail filled the air as the woman collapsed. Detective Young and the officer caught her before she hit the ground.

"I want to see him." She reached for Jake. "Please let me see him."

"I can't do that, but I will need you to make a formal identification later." Jake ran a hand through his hair. Emotions warred in his chest. He needed to focus on what he did best. "Detective Young will escort you to the police station." He turned and scanned the flashing lights. An ambulance sat at the curb and he jogged over to it. "I have a young woman who needs transportation to the hospital ASAP."

"We were sent to pick up the dead guy."

"I'll clear it. He can wait."

"You stay here and call in the change. We'll bring her out."

"Her name's Mackenzie Love." Jake pulled his phone from his pocket as the men rolled the gurney into the house.

Before he could punch any numbers, a call came through. The Chief.

"What's going on?" He growled. "And don't tell me we got a problem."

"Yes, sir." Jake walked several feet away from the commotion. "Quinton Underwood attacked Mac and Miss P at their office, and Miss P shot him."

"Oh, man. Is he dead?"

"Yes, sir."

"Are they hurt?"

"Mac is on her way to the hospital." The ambulance pulled away from the curb, sirens blaring. He waited until it was down the road. "Miss P has some scrapes and bruises, but nothing serious."

"Young called in about Francis. He told me how she was hanging around outside."

"Yes. She'd been following her dad. She expected him to do something stupid." Jake rubbed his left arm. It was beginning to ache. Too much activity.

"She should have come to us." The Chief's chair squeaked. "Make sure Mac is okay and then get back here. We still have to interview Thomas Underwood." He sighed. "And I guess now we have to let him know about his dad."

"Will do. Sir." Jake craved rest, but some food and an ibuprofen would have to do. And a few minutes with Mac before heading for the station. He motioned to an officer. "I need a ride to the hospital with a run through Wimpy's on the way."

At the hospital emergency room, Jake caught up with Mac in her room. "We gotta stop meeting like this. The staff know us by name."

"I know." Mac rolled her eyes and winced.

"How's your head?" Mac slowly turned and tilted her head so he could see where Quinton had pulled her hair out. His stomach roiled at the sight, and he sat down.

"Are you okay?" Mac faced him again.

He swallowed and nodded.

"The doctor thinks he can sew it up rather than have to do grafts."

Jake nodded again. He didn't see how, but he'd trust the experts.

"You don't look too sure." Mac eyed him.

"I'm a detective." He placed his hand on his chest. "Not a doctor." He rose. "And I need to get back. We still have to talk with Thomas Underwood."

"I was going to listen to the interview." Mac's face fell.

"I'll tell you all about it." He gave her a gentle kiss on the lips.

It was Mac's turn to nod.

He hated leaving her. "Where are you going from here?"

"Miss P's taking me back to Sam's and picking up Zoe."

"Good. Stay there and we'll talk in the morning." He raised an eyebrow at her. "Not an order, just a suggestion."

"In that case, I'll take it under advisement." She waved a hand at him. "You better go before you get in trouble."

The door opened, and a man in a white lab jacket bustled in, followed by a woman in blue scrubs. "Let's take care of your scalp injury, shall we?"

Time for Jake to exit. He caught the door before it closed and stepped into the hall. No way could he watch a doctor sew up Mac. Himself, sure, but not the woman he loved. Even the thought of what was going on in the room he'd left was enough to speed up his pace through the hospital and out the door.

He walked out from under the overhang into the open space of the parking lot and paused to draw in a lungful of brisk evening air. That was better. The aromas of garlic and exhaust fumes instead of antiseptics and recirculated air.

And then he remembered—he didn't have a car. He yanked his phone from his pocket and called for an officer to pick him up.

Fifteen minutes later, Jake took the elevator to the second floor. His arm ached and his headache was back. He needed more meds before talking to Underwood.

"I put Francis Underwood in the break room. There's a female officer with her." Vic Young followed Jake into his office. "How's Mac?"

"She's okay." Jake ran a hand over his hair. "The doc thinks he can sew her up."

"You don't look so good." Vic peered at him.

"Headache." Jake made a vague gesture toward his forehead. "And my arm hurts. I took something."

"Want a cup of coffee?"

"Yeah." Jake plopped into his chair.

"I'll be back." Vic left.

Jake put his head in his hand. What he wouldn't give for about two hours' sleep.

"I thought I saw you come in."

There was no mistaking that voice. Jake raised his gaze to his boss.

"You look like you been spit out of a whale." The Chief crossed his arms in front of his chest.

"That's a new one. Never heard that before."

"Just made it up. But it fits. Are you up to interviewing Thomas Underwood, or should I call Walker?"

Vic appeared behind the Chief.

"I'll be fine." Jake inclined his head toward Vic. "I'll drink some coffee, and we'll get started."

"You're sure?"

"Yes, sir." After all the work Mac had put into this case, he owed it to her. Besides, he'd started it and he meant to finish it.

After Chief Baker left, Jake chugged his coffee and threw the Styrofoam cup in the trash. *Lord, give me the strength and clarity of mind to do this.* He stood and gazed at Vic. "Ready?"

"After you." Vic stepped aside.

"You take the lead. I'll jump in with my questions." Jake paused outside the door to Interview Room One. "Okay?"

Vic nodded and opened the door. The tall gray-haired man inside paced, his hands stuffed in the pockets of his jeans.

"Take a seat, Mr. Underwood." Vic indicated which chair. "I'm Detective Victor Young. This is Detective Jake Sanders."

"May I ask why I'm here?" Thomas Underwood lowered himself onto the white plastic chair facing the camera.

"Before we get into that, I'm afraid we have some bad news for you." Vic sat across from him. "I'm sorry to tell you that your father is dead."

Thomas Underwood sat back. "Who killed him?"

"Why do you think he was killed?" Vic asked.

"Because he wasn't a very nice man." Underwood sighed. Bags rimmed his light gray eyes. "He and I never got along."

"I'm sorry to hear that. If you wish to postpone this interview, we can."

"No." He straightened. "I'm okay. I'd rather get this over with."

"What were you told when they picked you up?" Vic looked up from his file.

"They said something about attempted murder." Underwood ran a hand through his silver hair. "Am I under arrest?"

"No." Vic's voice turned to steel. "Not yet."

"I don't understand." Underwood shifted his anxious gaze from Vic to Jake and back. "Who am I supposed to have tried to murder?"

The detectives said nothing. Jake scanned Underwood's face. Either he was an outstanding actor, or he didn't have a clue what was going on.

"Oh no." The man's eyes widened, and he waved his hands in front of him. "No. You can't think that I had anything to do with Doug's ..." He furrowed his brow and turned his palms toward the ceiling. "What reason would I have?"

"The oldest one in the book. Greed."

"But Doug's business was making a great profit."

Underwood scooted to the edge of his chair. "I'd be a fool to hurt him."

"Unless he threatened to turn you in to the police for embezzling," Jake said in a low voice.

"Embezzling?" Underwood swiveled his gaze toward Jake. "Where'd you get that ridiculous idea?"

"Then you'd be fine with us going through your accounts for James Electric."

His face paled.

"I thought so." Jake shot a look at Vic. "Did Doug find out? Is that why you tried to electrocute him?"

"No." Underwood dragged a hand down his face. "I mean. He didn't know. But he was my friend. I didn't try to electrocute him."

"Then why did your sister tell Zachary Zane you needed the key to the fuse box room?"

"Francis ..." Underwood muttered under his breath. The lines in his face deepened into creases as he stared at the opposite wall.

"Did you use the key to get into the room and switch the fuses?" Vic asked.

No response. Thomas Underwood sat as if in a trance.

"Mr. Underwood." Jake stood. "Are you okay?" Had he had a stroke? That's all they'd need right now. Jake touched the man's shoulder. "Mr. Underwood."

Underwood jerked and focused on Jake. "You're right. I did it."

# CHAPTER 37

Jake studied the face of the man in front of him. It all made sense, but something nagged at his gut. "You switched the fuses."

Underwood averted his eyes and nodded.

Jake returned to his chair. Underwood slumped, the posture of a man who was relieved to get it off his chest. Or of a man resigned to his fate?

"What about Laura James?" Vic asked.

Underwood looked up sharply. He opened his mouth. Then snapped it shut. He nodded.

"I need to hear it for the tape."

"I ... killed Laura James." He placed his head in his hands. "God forgive me."

Vic turned to Jake. "Anything else we need?"

"Where's the gun?" Somehow, Jake knew the answer before it was given.

"I threw it in the river."

"Where?"

"I, um, don't remember."

"Okay." Vic stood. "This officer will read you your rights and the charges, and get you processed."

Jake rose. "Is there anything else you want to tell us, Mr. Underwood?" *Like what it is you're holding back.*

He shook his head. "I would like to speak to my sister."

"We'll see if that can be arranged."

In the hallway outside the room, Vic thumped Jake on his good shoulder. "We did it."

"Did we?" Jake pressed his lips together in a slight grimace. "I hope so."

"You're not convinced?"

He glanced back at the door to the interview room. "Don't you think he flipped awfully quick?"

"When he heard we knew about the key, he figured it was all over."

"Maybe."

"Speaking of which," Vic said. "I'll get his sister so he can talk to her before we put him in jail. She might be able to jog his memory about where he threw the gun into the river."

"I'll go with you." Jake couldn't shake the feeling that something didn't add up. Ahead, Vic entered the break room.

"What do you mean she left?" Vic's angry voice carried out into the hall.

"What's wrong?" Jake poked his head in the door.

"They let Francis Underwood leave." Vic waved an arm at the officers sitting at the table.

"We had no reason to detain her," one of the officers said. "What were we supposed to do?"

"You could have thought of something." Vic glared at them.

"Hey. It's okay." Jake steered Vic out of the room. "We'll pick her up again. No big deal." But the lump of disquiet inside him grew. "Let's go see the Chief and—" The hallway tilted and Jake stumbled.

"Whoa." Vic grabbed him by the arm. "You don't look so good. Let's get you somewhere to sit." He supported Jake to a chair inside his office.

"Thanks, man." Jake rubbed the back of his neck. Vic handed him an uncapped bottle of water, and he rolled it across his forehead before taking a drink.

"You need to go home. I'll get an officer to take you to Sam's," Vic said. "I'll brief the Chief and get out an APB on Francis Underwood."

Jake nodded. "Thanks."

The ride back to Sam's seemed to take five minutes. Probably because he fell into a deep sleep the moment the car started to move. At the house, he barely registered the officer getting Alan and the two of them helping him to his room. If Alan hadn't been there, Jake would have fallen into bed fully dressed, gun and all.

MAC CUT a look from her notes to the doorway. Was he going to sleep all day? She pushed her chair back. What happened last evening at Thomas Underwood's interview? The pain pills she took wiped her out, and apparently, Jake didn't get back until late.

"Don't you dare go knock on his door." Sam peered at her over the edge of her computer screen. "The man needs to rest."

"I wasn't." Mac glared back. "I was getting some more tea." She yanked the refrigerator door open.

"And stop being so noisy. It's not even nine o'clock yet."

Mac sighed. If her head didn't hurt so much, she'd have more patience. Maybe. She explored the edges of the bandage with her fingers. "When you get to a stopping point, would you help me change the dressing on my scalp?"

"Of course." Sam rose and gathered the bandages and tape. "Sit here in the light." She wet a clean paper towel with warm water and dabbed the crusty edges to loosen the gauze from the skin. "Let me know if this hurts."

With slow and gentle movements, she worked the tape off the skin and lifted the gauze away from the wound. "I can see it's healing already." She cleaned and dried the area around the stitches, placed a fresh gauze over it, and taped it down. "There. Do you need a pain pill?"

"No." Mac squeezed Sam's hand. "Thanks. You're going to be a great mother."

"I hope so." Sam rubbed her belly.

"You do a great job with me." Mac chuckled.

"Most of the time." Sam eased onto her chair.

"What are you doing?"

"When Jake came in last night, he told me to research Francis Underwood."

"Why?" Did Thomas confess? Did he implicate Francis? She gazed at the doorway, willing Jake to appear.

"I have no idea. I told you. He was so exhausted, he couldn't walk on his own. The officer and Alan had to help him into his room." Sam drew in a deep breath and let it out. "I pray he didn't cause himself more harm."

The idea that Jake would ever be that weak scared Mac, and she forgot about the interview. She dropped her head in prayer that a good night's sleep was all he needed to recover.

"Where can a guy get some breakfast around here?" Jake's voice, still muffled by sleep, sounded in the doorway.

Mac amended her prayer. A good night's sleep and some food. "I think that can be arranged." She jumped up and hugged him.

As she fixed eggs and bacon and toast, she cast appraising glances at her fiancé. Jake's brow creased in a pensive expression. Something was bothering him. "Here you are, my master."

"Thanks."

No comeback or banter. He hadn't heard her. She touched his shoulder. "What's up, Jake?"

"What?" He looked at her then, a smile on his lips.

"I asked what you're thinking about." She sat next to him.

"Nothing." He took a bite of egg.

"I'm researching Francis Underwood like you asked." Sam squinted at her computer screen.

Jake paused, his fork halfway to his mouth. "I didn't ask you to research Francis Underwood."

"Yes, you did." Sam's forehead pinched in the middle. "Last night. When you came in."

"I don't remember." Jake laid his fork down on his plate. "Did I say anything else?"

"No." Sam shook her head. "Just that."

He sat for a long moment before taking another bite.

Mac leaned back. So the something up with Jake had to do with Francis Underwood. But what? "We heard you took Francis down to the police station. What was she doing at my office last evening?"

"We did." Jake turned his gaze on her. "She said she was following her dad because she was worried he'd do something bad. But she left before we could talk to her."

"Why would she walk out like that?" Frustration sparked Mac's nerves.

"Did she give a positive ID for Quinton Underwood?" Sam asked.

"Don't know. We asked her to." Jake pushed his plate of half-eaten breakfast aside. "Thomas Underwood wants to speak to her."

"How did that go?" Mac's attention snapped back to her original desire, and she pulled her notepad in front of her.

"He confessed to the attempted murder of Douglas James and the murder of Laura James." Jake pulled on his earlobe.

"You don't seem satisfied." Mac gave him a questioning gaze.

"It all fits together. But, until we told him about Francis going to Zane for the key to the electrical room, Underwood vehemently denied doing anything. After, he did a one-eighty and confessed to everything."

Jake searched Mac's gaze as if she might have the answer. She held his gaze while her brain processed what he'd told her. "Could there be two people? One who tried to kill Doug? And one who killed Laura?"

Jake nodded. "But who?"

"Laura could have tried to kill Doug. Maybe she told Francis to get the key and she would give it to Thomas."

"Too far-fetched."

Even as she said it, Mac knew it wouldn't work. Thomas had to be the one who went after Doug. But as for Laura, the three original suspects all seemed good to her. Thomas, Francis, or Mrs. Green.

"I think I found something that will interest you guys." Sam beamed at them over her computer. "Francis Underwood is not a nurse."

# CHAPTER 38

Mac stared at her friend. "Francis didn't go to nursing school?"

"She went." Sam tipped her head toward the screen. "She didn't finish."

"Is that relevant to the case?" Jake asked.

Mac shrugged. "She's been telling everyone she's a nurse. I mean. Even at the hospital, she got special privileges to see Doug because they thought she was one of them." Mac made a note to ask Mrs. White what she knew.

Sam scrolled down the information on the screen and whistled. "If I'm reading this correctly, our girl got in some kind of trouble, and that's why she had to leave nursing school."

"What was she supposed to have done?" Mac leaned on the table.

"I can't tell."

Unease slithered through her stomach. "I think it's time I called Beth."

"Your older sister?" Jake asked. "Why?"

"She knew Francis in school. Maybe she can give us some more information."

"Good idea." He ran a hand over his chin. "I need a shave."

"I'll let Killer out." Sam stood and stretched. "Then I'll keep digging."

"I can take care of Killer." Mac rose. "I'll call my sister while I'm outside." She pulled on her jacket and went into Sam and Alan's bedroom. "I bet you're ready to stretch your legs." She unlatched the door to his crate and the beautiful golden dog bounded out.

He stood on his back legs and Mac took hold of his front paws. "I know. You love me." She pushed him down. "Sit." He planted his rear on the floor, but when she bent to put his harness on him, he stretched his neck to try to lick her face.

Mac ducked his kisses and laughed. "I love you too." And she did. Every time she looked at him, she remembered how he almost died trying to protect her best friend. Killer held a very special place in her heart. She clicked the leash onto his harness. "Let's see your mom before we go outside."

Mac followed Killer over to where Sam was sitting. "I don't know how you manage. He's about to pull me off my feet."

"He behaves for me." Sam ruffled his ears. "Don't you, big guy?" She touched her nose to his. "He's my buddy."

The dog looked at Sam with adoration.

"Now, go outside with Mac and behave." She shook her finger at him. "I'll see you in a little bit."

He trotted over to the back door and looked at Mac as if to say, "Are you coming?"

Mac shook her head. Sam was truly amazing.

Once outside, she removed Killer's leash and let him roam the fenced-in yard while she sat at the table on the patio. A cool wind still blew from the north, but it wasn't bad. Mac took out her phone and pressed the buttons for Beth's number.

"Calling before noon. Are you okay?" Beth's voice sounded tinged with concern.

"I'm fine." Mac itched to jump right to the reason she called, but remembered her manners. "How are all of you?"

"We're getting over the flu. I'm okay, but your oldest nephew is still under the weather."

"Tell him if he doesn't get better, Auntie Mac will have to come give him kisses and hugs."

"I'm sure that will do the trick." Beth laughed. "Okay. So what are you really calling about?"

"You know me too well." Mac sighed. "Do you remember a girl named Francis Underwood?"

"Vaguely. I knew her brother, Thomas, better."

Mac scanned the yard. Where was Killer? "Hang on a sec." She stood and held the phone away from her. "Killer, come here, boy."

The dog came loping up the yard from behind some bushes in the back.

"Where are you?" Beth's tiny voice sounded from next to her.

"Sorry." Mac replaced the phone to her ear. "I'm at Sam's. I took her dog out for some exercise, and I was afraid he'd gotten out of the yard." Mac threw a stick and watched the dog bound away. "What were you saying about Francis?"

"She was in Kate's class at school. I was friends with her brother."

Killer dropped the stick at her feet and yipped at her. She picked it up and threw it again.

"What can you tell me about Thomas?"

"Why do you want to know?"

Mac threw the stick once more. "He's suspected of trying to kill his partner, Doug James."

"I don't believe it." Beth's tone held a scoff. "The Thomas I knew wouldn't hurt anyone. In fact, he went out of his way to keep the peace. He was that kind of guy."

"The evidence says—"

"I don't care what your evidence says. This time, you've got it wrong, baby sister. Mark my words."

"Okay." Mac tossed the wet stick again and wiped her hands on her jeans. "But you never heard anything about his sister, Francis?"

"There was something, but I can't remember the details. You need to call Kate. She'd know."

"Thanks, Beth. Listen, don't tell anyone what we've talked about. I'm serious, Beth."

"Okay." Puzzlement sounded in Beth's voice. "If you say so. But someday you owe me an explanation."

"I will. I promise." Mac looked down to see Killer lying at her feet, the stick drooping from his mouth. He'd given up on her. "Sorry, boy." She clipped his leash back on and opened the back door.

"Back so soon?" Sam raised her gaze from her computer screen.

"He got tired of playing fetch." Mac bent to wipe the goldendoodle's muddy feet.

He swiped her cheek with his rough tongue.

"Thanks for the kiss." She grabbed a clean towel and wiped her face. "Go see your mom." She let him loose.

The big dog bounded across the room to his water bowl and lapped noisily. The tags on his collar jingled as he shook the excess from his fur and trotted over to Sam. He laid his head on her leg.

"Did you talk to Beth?" Sam ran a hand down Killer's silky head.

"I did, but Francis wasn't in her grade. Thomas was. And, according to her, he wouldn't have tried to kill Doug. I didn't even talk to her about Laura." Mac soaped her hands at the kitchen sink.

"Did she know anything about Francis?"

"No." Mac washed, rinsed, and dried her hands on a dishtowel. "She said I should call Kate. She would know more."

"While you were outside, Miss P called." Sam joined Mac at the sink. "The police are finished at the office, and she's going over to start putting it back together. I thought I might go over and help."

"No. You can't."

Jake's voice sounded behind them.

"I saw the office, and it's a wreck." He glared at Sam from the doorway. "Too many chances for you to trip and fall. Alan would never forgive me."

"You have nothing to say about what I do." Sam's eyes flashed. "And Alan respects my ability to take care of myself."

"That's true." Mac placed a hand on her arm. "But at this point, there's not much you can do. We're going to need Leonard or somebody to help us get the furniture back where it belongs before we can start on the smaller things." She nodded at Sam's computer. "You'd be more useful here doing what you do best. Investigation."

"I do have more sites I want to look at concerning Francis and Thomas Underwood." She pointed at her brother, her face still rigid with anger. "But don't think I'm staying home because *you* said I should. It's *my* decision."

"I understand." Jake held his hand up in surrender.

Mac shook her head at him. When would he learn? "I'll drive you to the police station if you're ready."

"Yeah." He crossed the kitchen and kissed Sam on the cheek. "I love you, Sis."

"I love you too." She gave him a quick hug. "But I wish you'd stop being so bossy."

"I'll try." He slid his eyes to Mac.

"I'll swing by the office and see if we can't get help with the furniture. When we get to the file organization, I'll call." Mac pulled on her coat.

Sam nodded, already engrossed in her computer.

Outside, Jake put a hand on Mac's arm. "I meant what I said to Sam for you too. I'll try to stop giving you orders."

Mac touched his cheek. "Thanks, but it's pretty ingrained in who you are. I think this may be one of those things we'll be fussing about most of our lives."

"You don't think I can change?" Jake climbed into the passenger seat.

Mac started the car before she answered. Did she want him to change? That was the real question. How would changing how he reacts to her putting herself into a dangerous situation change the rest of his personality? Would he stop caring about other things? "I fell in love with you the way you are. I'm not sure I want you to change."

"Now I'm confused. What do you want?"

"Let's just leave things the way they are." She threw him a smile. "You be you, and I'll be me. Even if it means butting heads once in a while."

"I'm good with that." He leaned over and kissed her. "What about Sam?"

Mac laughed. "You'll have to make your own deal with your sister. I'm staying out of that one."

"Thanks a lot." He chuckled. "Changing the subject. What did Beth tell you about Francis?"

"Nothing." Mac waited for a car to cross in front of her. "But she told me in no uncertain terms that we had arrested the wrong man for attempted murder. Thomas Underwood would not have tried to kill Doug James."

"How does she know?"

"He's too nice."

"Aw, the old too nice defense. Of course. Well, I guess that settles that. I'll release him as soon as I get to the station." Sarcasm dripped from every word.

"I'm sure you will." She stopped in front of the glass doors to the building housing the police station. "She told me to call Kate about Francis. I plan on doing so later."

"Let me know what you find out." He unbuckled, leaned across for another kiss, and levered himself out of the car. "Be careful, Mac. I love you."

"Always." She blew him a kiss. "I love you too." It still pained her to see him—the man she thought of as indestructible—with a bandaged shoulder. Like an eagle with a broken wing. Tears welled in the backs of her eyes as she watched him go, the earlier sense of foreboding forming a lump in her throat. Almost as if this would be the last time she would see him.

# CHAPTER 39

Mac punched Kate's phone number and let it ring four times. When voicemail picked up, she pressed End without leaving a message. Her middle sister led a busy life. With twin girls in middle school, it seemed she was always on the go.

The three sisters were very close, despite Beth and Kate being born five years apart, with another eight years before Mac came along. Once, Mac asked her mother if she'd had trouble getting pregnant, but she told her youngest daughter she'd planned it that way on purpose so she could spend time with each of her babies.

Mac was the only one to stay in Washington. Beth and Kate both moved about four hours away to Kansas City with their families.

Disappointment washed over her. She'd counted on her sister's positive outlook to help her overcome lingering anxiety. But she'd try again later. In the meantime, she'd have to find a way out of her gloom on her own.

At the office, a ripple of joy coursed through Mac at the

sight of Miss P's large sedan and Zoe's sport utility vehicle. Her two friends were just the antidote she needed. And, the three of them should be able to make real progress at getting the office back in shape.

The sky opened up and rain fell in heavy sheets.

"Where did that come from?" Mac pulled her umbrella from between the seats in her car. Should she wait for it to pass or brave the deluge and make a run for it? "I won't melt." She opened her door, stuck her umbrella outside, and pressed the button.

By the time she gained the shelter of the porch, her shoes were soaked, and her teeth were chattering. She tried the door. Locked. She had a key, but doubted she could stop shaking enough to use it. "Open the door. It's freezing out here."

"Mackenzie." Miss P flung open the door and pulled her in. "Why didn't you call first?"

"I-I-did-didn't-think-about-it." She couldn't stop shivering.

"Sit here." Miss P took Mac's wet jacket and hung it on the coat rack. She wrapped her heavy wool coat around Mac. "I'll make you some hot tea."

"Man." Zoe handed her some gloves. "That rain came out of nowhere. And the temperature dropped too. We're lucky it's not ice."

Mac pulled on the gloves and nodded. Miss P placed a steaming cup of tea before her. She wrapped both hands around it and bent over to inhale the aroma. The shivering stopped. She straightened and scanned the room. It was not a pretty sight.

Every cushion and pillow of their reception room furniture had been slashed. Drawers were smashed against side tables and the walls. Files and their contents covered the floor. Nothing remained on the walls, including the antique mirror, which lay shattered into a hundred sparkling shards at the end of the room. Mac's spirit sank, and all she wanted was to go home and sleep.

"We've managed to right the conference table and rescue seven chairs so far." Miss P ran a finger along a new scratch on the table top. "I believe the damage here can be taken care of with a good polishing." She placed a hand on a chair. "These chairs seem sturdy, but the other three will need to be reglued."

"We'll need new reception furniture." Mac let out a sigh.

"Yes, we will. I've already contacted the supplier."

"Now's our chance to get a couple of those chairs like we sat in at that office." Zoe snapped her fingers. "You know. What's his name?"

"Thomas Underwood." Mac raised her eyebrows at her.

"Yeah." Zoe pointed at her. "Remember how cool they were?"

They were nice, but Mac had other priorities right now. "Talk to Miss P."

"Thanks." Zoe's eyes lit up.

Mac rose and hung Miss P's coat on the rack. "Here. Thanks, Zoe." She handed the gloves back to Zoe. "I'm going into my office to make a call. I won't be long." She picked up her mug of tea and left the room. Time to try Kate again.

"Hi, baby sis." Kate's voice was as golden and warm as the sun. "Sorry I wasn't able to take your call earlier. I was in a meeting."

"I figured." Her middle sister always made her smile. "It's fine."

"I talked to Beth, and she filled me in on your talk last night. So I guess you're calling me about Francis Underwood?"

"I am." Mac paused. "But first I'd like to know how you and your hubby and kids are doing."

"We're fine. Just the usual teenage drama. This one accuses the other one of wearing her favorite sweater without asking." Kate's tinkling laugh sounded. "You remember."

"I remember you and Beth fighting over clothes. I was too young to get into that."

"Excuse me, but what about my college sweatshirt that went missing?"

"I have no idea how that got into my closet." Mac chuckled.

"Uh-huh." Kate snorted her disbelief. "Listen, I could reminisce all day, but I have another appointment this morning. What do you want to know about Francis?"

"What do you remember?"

"She had anger issues, and the kids at high school were afraid of her."

"Did she ever hurt anyone?" Mac pulled a fresh notepad out of her desk.

"I remember one time. She was accused of pushing a guy down the stairs at school," Kate said. "She claimed it was an accident and apologized profusely, but ..."

"But what?"

"Well, the guy who fell was the one she'd asked to the Sadie Hawkins dance. He'd turned her down and accepted an invitation from someone else. When he broke his leg in the fall, the girl he was going with backed out on him, so Francis stepped up and said she'd be glad to take him. Wheelchair and all."

"Did he go with her?"

"Yes, but some of my friends said he told the guys he was afraid if he didn't, she'd hurt him again. Only worse."

Icy fingers slid down Mac's spine.

"Francis disappeared after that, and the gossip was that she was in St. Louis at a psychiatric hospital."

"But later she was accepted to nursing school." Mac doodled a question mark on her pad.

"I never could figure that one out." Beth sighed. "I did hear she didn't finish, and I'm not surprised."

"But you don't know why."

"No. I can try to find out if you want?"

Mac pondered the question, but something inside her kept telling her to keep her sisters out of this. "No. Don't ask anyone about Francis. In fact, don't mention that I called you about her. I mean it, Kate. I'm serious about this."

"I get it." Kate's tone had lost its sunshine. "Mac, be careful. We may not say it often, but Beth and I love you very much."

"I love you guys too."

After Mac finished her call with Kate, she made a list of facts to check about Francis Underwood. Did she spend time in a psychiatric hospital in St. Louis? If so, which one? And why? How did she get admitted to nursing school? And why was she kicked out? Between Miss P and Sam, she was confident they could find the answers.

She stood and crossed to her office door. Three women's voices sounded in the room beyond. Two she recognized. One she didn't. She stepped into the main room. Miss P and Zoe sat facing her, their hands folded on the table. A third woman sat with her back to Mac.

Zoe raised a terrified gaze to Mac. The woman swiveled in her chair. "So pleased you could join us." Francis Underwood motioned Mac over. A cellphone sat on the table in front of her, and she held a twenty-two revolver in her hand.

# CHAPTER 40

A strange air of peace blanketed Mac. The moment she had been dreading was finally here. *Lord, guide my actions and give me the right words.* "Francis." Mac let out a sigh. "What are you doing?"

The question took the woman by surprise. She opened her mouth to answer, but nothing came out.

"She's here to find out what happened to her father." Miss P spoke in a low, sad tone.

"Okay." Mac pulled out a chair. "What do you want to know?"

"Why did he come here? What did he want?" She flitted her eyes between Mac and Miss P. Eyes that were at once hard and cruel yet deeply wounded.

"He demanded—at gunpoint—any evidence we might have proving he killed Mackenzie's parents." Miss P peered at the woman over her glasses. "When I told him the files were at my home, but that we had copies in the safe, he insisted we get them."

"My father killed your parents?" Francis faced Mac. "He must have had a good reason. What was it?"

For a moment, uncertainty flashed in Francis's eyes. Perhaps beneath all that anger and turmoil lay a place of reason that Mac could tap into. "Your father stole money from my parents. When they found out, they turned him in, and he went to prison for a while."

"So they were the reason I lost my daddy." Rage flared on her face once more. "And when he came here, you killed him." She raised the revolver.

"Actually, I killed Quinton Underwood," Miss P said in a firm voice.

Francis pointed the gun at the older woman. Mac sprang from her chair, but Francis anticipated her move. She grabbed her phone and leaped to her feet.

"Sit down." Francis waved the revolver around at all of them. "I don't really care who pulled the trigger. I'd already decided to kill anyone who was here." She held up her phone. "I've got a bomb hidden in the house linked to my cellphone."

"A bomb?" Zoe bent to look under the table. "Where?"

"Sit still, child." Miss P placed a hand on her arm.

Mac's chest ached. What had she gotten her high school friend into? And her beloved Miss P? If only she hadn't gone after who killed her parents ...

"Mackenzie, it's not your fault." Miss P gazed at her with loving eyes.

Oh, Miss P. Mac licked her lips. *Lord, we need Your help.* "So it was you who blew up the house where Zane was and killed his sister?"

A question crossed Francis's face so fast that if Mac hadn't been focused on it, she would have missed it.

"Yes."

"Zane made it out. He's at the police station. That's how we know it was you who asked for the key."

She paled a little.

"But you don't have to worry. Thomas has confessed to everything."

"What do you mean?" Francis stepped closer to Mac.

"I mean he told the police he tried to kill Doug and also shot Laura." Mac eased herself away from the table. "How do you know so much about bombs anyway?" Out of the corner of her eye, she saw Miss P leave her chair and move around behind Francis.

"You'd be surprised what you learn from ..." Francis gave an evil grin. "Let's just say I've met some very colorful people in my life."

"How does this one work? I mean. If I'm going to die, you could at least let me know that much." Mac moved an inch so Francis had to angle away from what was going on behind her.

"First, I'll secure all of you—" She glanced toward Zoe and Miss P. "Where's Miss—"

Miss P grabbed Francis's arms and yanked them down. The gun went off. Mac leaped across, yanked the phone from her grasp, and threw it across the room. Miss P held onto her gun hand.

"I'm afraid she's too strong for me." Miss P cried.

"I've got her." Zoe levered Francis's thumb back. There was an audible crack, and Francis screamed as she dropped the gun.

"Miss P, call the police and bomb squad." Mac pulled Francis's left arm around behind her back and shoved her against the wall. "Zoe, go in the kitchen and get the plastic restraints. Third drawer down on the left."

"Got it."

"Calm down." Mac put as much authority as she could muster into her voice.

Francis stilled. She was about the same size as Mac but without the muscle tone. But what she didn't have in strength, she made up for in passion bordering on mania. Mac prayed she'd spent her fervor for the time being.

Without warning, she yelled with rage and threw her head back, smashing into the bridge of Mac's nose. The pain sent shock waves through Mac's body and Francis tore her arm from Mac's hands.

Instead of running, the woman turned and reached for Mac's throat. Mac threw an arm up to block her. But she was strong. Francis's all-consuming rage added superhuman strength to her attack. How long would Mac be able to hold her off?

Mac kicked at Francis's knee. The woman tilted to the side, but maintained her pressure. Where were Miss P and Zoe? She tried to scream, but blood from her nose clogged her throat.

Francis roared and drove herself forward with renewed fury. Mac's arm gave and Francis clamped her hand around Mac's throat.

Mac couldn't breathe. She tore at Francis's grip with her fingers. Was this the reason she felt she'd never see Jake again? *Lord, no.*

A yell sounded above the roaring in her ears.

A blur to her right, a sound her oxygen-deprived brain couldn't place, and the vise on her throat released. She slumped to the ground, drew in a deep breath, and coughed.

Mac's vision cleared in time to see Zoe rush Francis headfirst like an enraged bull. The woman flew backward and bounced off the wall. A lamp with a heavy marble bottom sat within reach. She swung it at Zoe's head.

Miss P deflected the blow with a broom handle to Francis's

arm. Zoe spun out of range. The enraged woman threw the lamp at Miss P and raced for the front door.

"You fools. You're not safe yet." With a look of pure evil, Francis slammed the door behind her.

By the time Zoe got to the porch, the woman had disappeared.

"The police and bomb squad should be here any minute." Miss P handed Mac a bottle of water. "Are you hurt, Mackenzie?"

She took a gulp. "I think I'm going to need more stitches." She touched her nose. "And maybe new ones on my head." Mac coughed again. "What do you think she meant by we're not safe yet?"

"I believe she was referring to the bomb." Miss P folded her hands in front of her.

# CHAPTER 41

Mac got her legs under her and pushed to her feet. The pounding in her head threatened to bring her to her knees once more, but she managed to stagger to a chair by the table. And boy, was she glad she did. The first person through the door was Jake, and he didn't look happy.

At least this time, there was no dead body.

He strode over to her. "This is the second time I've found you with your face covered in blood."

"But this time it's my own."

He bent to examine her nose. "Ouch. A head butt?"

She nodded.

He started to run a hand down her hair, but stopped. "I'm sorry, sweetheart."

She raised her damp gaze to his. "It only hurts when I breathe."

He scratched his forehead and glanced around. "Let me get you some help. Then we can talk."

Another visit to the ER. "Can't I ride in a squad car? Do I need an ambulance for a broken nose?"

"I've got to stay here. I'm in charge of the scene." He rubbed the back of his neck. "I don't like the idea of you going to the hospital without me, but you need to get your nose looked at right away. Or you'll end up with a bump like mine".

Last thing she wanted was matching nose bumps. "We can catch up later."

"Wait here. I'll get someone to take you." He left, but returned soon with a woman officer in tow. "I'd like you to take Miss Love to the hospital emergency room. She has a broken nose and would prefer a car to an ambulance."

"Yes, sir." She smiled at Mac. "I'm Officer Rhonda Hudson."

"I'm Mac." She gave a quick upturn of her mouth. "I think I'll need help to your car."

"No problem." Rhonda placed a sturdy arm around Mac's waist and took her hand. "Here we go."

Mac glanced around inside the patrol car. No candy wrappers or fast food bags anywhere. "You're very neat."

Rhonda laughed. "I try. It's hard to keep it clean. The people we transport don't have a lot of respect for other people's property. If you know what I mean."

"I can imagine."

The officer cut her eyes to Mac. "How'd you break your nose?"

"Head butt from a very angry woman."

"Ahh." Rhonda nodded as if she totally understood. "Where is she now?"

"She got away." Her throat closed again, this time gripped by the icy hand of reality. Francis was still out there somewhere.

Rhonda stopped at the stop sign and started forward. "I'm sure—"

A car barreled out of nowhere from their right. The impact

sent a shock wave through her body and the sound reverberated through the cold March air. Mac's head hit the passenger window as the police car spun out of control.

In a matter of seconds, the car stopped. Francis Underwood swung a hammer at Mac's window. The safety glass shattered into a thousand pieces. She stuck her hand inside the car and opened the door.

Officer Hudson jumped from the car. "Police. I order you to stop."

"It's time to finish what I started." The woman yanked Mac by the arms. "Get out."

Officer Hudson drew her baton and hit Francis on the neck. The woman crumpled to the pavement. Hudson peered at Mac. "Is this the woman who attacked you earlier?"

Mac nodded.

Hudson handcuffed Francis and secured her in the back of the squad car, then reported the accident and attack to the police station.

Relief poured through Mac. Maybe now the killing would stop and they could relax.

Until a muffled boom shook her to her core. She looked at Officer Hudson. "We have to go back."

"I can't leave, but I'll call for another car."

"I warned you." Francis's sing-song voice came from the back seat of the patrol car.

Mac phoned Jake, Miss P, and Zoe in quick succession. No answer from any of them. "No, Lord, please. I can't have lost all of them. Please, not even one." Mac collapsed onto the passenger's seat of the patrol car and prayed. Sirens filled the midday air.

Her phone lit up. "Miss P. What ... how ..." Mac couldn't find the words.

"We're all safe, Mackenzie." Her friend's soothing voice sounded in her ear. "The bomb squad found the device under the house. Fortunately, we had time to move far enough away, but there was an auxiliary timer on it that didn't leave enough time to defuse it."

"The office?" The house was more than an office to Mac. Childhood memories of visiting her uncle at the house on Second Avenue and Johnson filled her mind. "Is it completely gone?"

"A good portion of it was destroyed by the bomb. It remains to be seen what will be standing after they put out the fire. I'm so sorry, Mackenzie."

Mac put her head in her hands. "At least no one was hurt." She would grieve for her memories later.

"We'll get through this, my dear." Miss P swallowed. "Are you at the hospital?"

"No." Mac raised her gaze as two more police cars arrived. "It's a long story. I'll tell you later. You concentrate on things there for me, will you?"

"Of course." Worry edged Miss P's words. "Be careful, Mackenzie."

"Always." But that was getting harder and harder to do. Was it time for her to marry Jake and find a different job? One that didn't involve guns and car wrecks and bombs? She'd think about it after she slept for a few days.

"This officer will take you back." Officer Rhonda Hudson indicated a young man in uniform.

"Actually, I'm ready to go to the hospital. I talked to Miss P and everybody is good." She dug a small smile out for the officers. "I'd rather get my nose taken care of."

"Whatever you want, Miss Love." The officer led her to his car. "You know, you're kind of a legend around the precinct."

"I am?"

"Yes, ma'am." He opened the door for her. "You're fearless and have a real talent for detective work. All the officers admire you."

"Thanks. I appreciate hearing that more than I can tell you." Mac gazed out the side window. *Okay, Lord, I hear You.*

# CHAPTER 42

Jake arrived at the station house in time to see Francis Underwood escorted in by two officers. In fact, the whole building knew when she hit the door. Her ear-piercing screams penetrated even the thickest walls.

"I want to see my brother. Thomas, I'm here. Where are you?"

"Be quiet," Jake roared at her.

Stunned, she clamped her mouth shut.

"You will get to see your brother." Jake lowered his voice to a growl. "But first, we have some questions for you."

"I'm not answering any questions until I see Thomas."

He gave her his best stony policeman stare and was pleased to see the muscles below her eyes twitch. "Questions first."

"You promise I'll see my brother?"

"I already did." He turned on his heel and led the way to Interview Room One. "This is Detective Victor Young. He will be joining us." Jake lifted his chin in Vic's direction.

The officer fastened Francis's handcuffs to the chair and walked to the corner of the room.

She yanked on the cuff. "Is this necessary? Three big strong men and you feel the need to cuff me to the chair?"

"It's procedure when we're dealing with a violent suspect." Jake opened the file on his lap. "And from the looks of this, you can get pretty physical at times."

"Only when I'm being attacked." She shrugged her free shoulder. "What do you expect me to do?"

"Pushing a boy down the steps because he turned you down for a Sadie Hawkins dance? You call that attacking you?"

Francis's neck reddened, but she closed her eyes and took a couple of deep breaths. "I didn't push him. He fell."

"That's not what he told his buddies. He said he went to the dance with you because he was afraid if he didn't, you'd hurt him worse." Jake studied her.

"That's not true. We had a good time." Her eyes glistened with unshed tears.

"Okay." He dropped his gaze to his notes. "Why did you disappear from high school?"

"I think you already know the answer to that one." The words seemed to slither from her mouth like a serpent.

Jake looked up sharply, his heart pounding in his chest. He wouldn't have been surprised to see the woman before him changed into some sort of hideous crone. But she looked the same. "Remind me."

"My parents—although I'm pretty sure it was my mother and not my father—had me committed to a psychiatric hospital in St. Louis. They diagnosed me with some stupid mental disorder and gave me medicine." Again, she shrugged. "I played along. Pretended to get better and take my meds so I could move back home." She gave a mirthless laugh. "The only good thing I got from my time there was to learn some valuable skills." She grinned at Jake. "Like bomb making. How is your shoulder by the way?"

Jake kept his gaze on his notes and concentrated on relaxing his grip on his pencil.

"His shoulder is fine," Vic said. "I may walk with a slight limp if that makes you happy."

"Oh." Francis shifted her gaze to Vic. "I didn't realize you were there too."

"Yep. And I talked to your brother earlier."

Now Vic had her full attention. Jake studied the woman. He understood a possible motive for Thomas Underwood to have tried to kill Doug James, but what reason could his sister have? Was she in on the embezzling? He doubted it. He couldn't see Thomas Underwood entrusting his sister with his secret crime. Did she find out and want to protect him? Possible, but not likely.

"I don't care what he said, Thomas didn't do it." She strained against her handcuff. "He's innocent."

"Then who did?" Vic asked.

Francis's eyes flitted around like two birds trapped in a cage. "Is Doug still alive?"

"He's still in a coma," Vic said. "If you call that alive."

"I want to see him." She bent forward, eyes pleading with the detectives. "I want to tell him the truth. To his face. Before he ... passes."

"You know who did this to him?"

"Yes, but I'll only tell it to him. You can record it, but I want to be the one to tell him." Tears pooled in her eyes. "I love him."

Jake shared a look with Vic. This was a first. But if it would get the confession they needed, that's all that mattered. "We'll see what we can do."

The detectives left the room and made a beeline for the Chief's office.

After briefing Chief Baker on what had happened, they hit

him with their plan to take Francis to the hospital to visit Doug and get her confession.

"This is the craziest thing I ever heard." The Chief ran a hand over his bald head. "Let me check with the lawyers to see if it will hold up in court." He punched in some numbers on his phone. "Not that she can't recant it later like they all do."

Jake checked his phone for text messages from Mac. None yet. He wanted to be with her when she went to see what remained of her office.

The Chief hung up. "Okay. It's all right as long as you make sure to read Miss Underwood her rights and state the usual precautions for the tape." He handed Jake a short list of items that had to be covered for the confession to be used in a court of law. "Here. Just as a reminder."

"I've been doing this for a while now, Chief." Jake stood.

"Yeah, but this one's a little unusual." Chief Baker waved a finger at the paper. "Be sure to get something on tape about the Laura James murder too."

"Yes, Chief ..."

"And make sure there are three or four of you in the room." The Chief stood and leaned on his desk. "I don't want any he-said-she-said problems."

"Yes, sir." Jake nodded at Vic. "Young will be there along with two other officers."

"Good." The Chief sat and pulled on his ear. "I can think of a million ways this could go sideways."

"It'll be fine. I'll let you know when we're on our way back."

Jake led the way back to the interview room. Inside, he motioned for the officer to release Francis Underwood from the chair and handcuff her hands together once more. "You and your partner will transport Miss Underwood to the hospital.

Detective Young and I will meet you there. We'll go through the Emergency Room door. Got that?"

"Yes, sir." The officer ushered Francis out of the room.

"Let's go." Jake held the door for Vic.

In the parking lot, Jake and Vic waited to get into their SUV until Francis Underwood was secured in the backseat of the squad car. Satisfied, they got in, belted up, and Vic backed out.

He didn't like this. He agreed with the Chief. Too many things could go wrong. And his experience had been that if something could go wrong, it would. "We need to be alert. This woman is smart and she's wily."

"Yeah. I'm nervous about this whole situation." Vic followed the squad car into the hospital parking lot and stopped right behind it. "I still can't figure out her motive."

"Me either." Jake massaged a spot above his right eye. "I think we can leave the cars here." He heaved himself out of the SUV and joined the others. "Ready?"

The officers each took one of Francis's arms and escorted her into the hospital and up the elevator to Doug James's room. Jake and Vic brought up the rear.

At the door, Francis hesitated. "Do I have to wear these handcuffs in there? In front of Doug?" She turned pleading eyes on Vic.

"Yes, Miss Underwood." Vic's arctic tone left no doubt. He was not a weak link that she could use to get her way.

"It was worth a try." She winked at him.

Jake turned to the officer guarding the door. "Do not let anyone in until I tell you it's okay. That includes nurses and doctors."

"Yes, sir."

He held the door while the small entourage passed through.

For a moment, every eye in the room was focused on the man

in the bed before them. Doug James lay with his arms outside the blanket. Tubes ran from his nose, mouth, and needles protruding from both arms. Wires snaked from under the covers and from electrodes attached to his temples and forehead. Machines whirred and clicked on both sides of his bed. His chest rose and fell to one of the mechanical rhythms. Yet he was oblivious. Peaceful.

"Oh, Doug. What have I done?" Francis surged forward as if to throw herself on the motionless form in the bed.

The two officers tightened their grips and moved her out of reach.

"Sit down." Jake scooted a wooden armchair to one side of the bed by Doug's feet. "Handcuff her to the chair on both sides." He started the recorder and listed all the people present in the room.

"We're in the hospital room of Douglas James, a coma patient, and the victim of attempted murder." He went on to explain why they were there and what they hoped to learn. Francis was read her rights, and it was time to begin.

"Miss Underwood, did you switch the fuses at the historic museum in an attempt to kill Douglas James?" Jake concentrated on her face.

Tears swam in her eyes. "No." She lifted her hand toward Doug to the limit of her cuff.

A flash flood of anger and frustration short-circuited Jake's hearing. Francis was still speaking. "Say that again, please."

"I said, I did switch the fuses, but I wasn't trying to kill Doug." She leaned forward as far as she could, her eyes fixed on Doug's face. "I love you. But you never even looked at me. I thought if I could do something so that you needed my help, then maybe ..." She turned her face to the ceiling. "He was only supposed to get shocked. Then I'd come in and treat his burn, and we'd look into each other's eyes, and he'd see me. Really see me." She gazed at the still face on the pillow before her. "And love me."

Jake averted his eyes. Sometimes the tragedy he ran up against was almost too much to bear. "But you didn't know he has atrial fibrillation."

"No. My brother didn't tell me until it was too late."

"But it didn't stop there," Vic said. "You may not have realized what would happen with Doug, but you sure knew what you were doing when you set the bomb at Zane's sister's house."

"I got scared." She raised red-rimmed eyes to his. "I'm not stupid. I knew Zane would get caught and tell you who got the key from him."

"But a bomb?" Vic's voice rose in anger. "You almost killed four policemen with it, as well as Zane and his sister."

"How was I to know you'd be there?" She jerked her hands against the restraints.

"That's not the point." Vic lowered his voice. "Are you going to tell Doug what happened to his wife?"

Francis paled. She glanced once more at the man in the hospital bed. "Do I have to?"

"I'm afraid so."

She drew in a deep breath and faced Doug. "Laura was going to shut off all your life support machines. I couldn't let her do that. So I shot her."

"You killed her," Vic said.

Francis nodded.

Jake looked up from his notes. "You need to say it for the tape."

"I killed her. Okay?" Francis yelled. "There. You happy?"

"No." Jake sighed. "Two innocent people are dead, with others recovering from injuries. A third is in a coma on life support. All because you wanted the attention of a married man.”

“Laura didn't love him.” Francis hissed. “I loved him—love him. He was going to get a divorce anyway.”

“So that makes it all okay?” Jake asked.

“Well, actually, it wasn't my fault. If Thomas had told me about his AFib, I never would have switched the fuses in the first place.”

“Are you saying it's all Thomas's fault?” Jake narrowed his eyes at her in disbelief.

“Yes.” She gave them a triumphant look.

When Jake, Vic, and the two officers guarding Francis got to the lobby of the emergency room, a familiar profile stood by the door with her back to him. "Mac?"

She turned toward him, and he winced inwardly at the bandage marring her beautiful face.

"Justh finisthed." She swept her gaze over the group.

The packing in her nose gave her voice a low-pitched twang, and Jake bit his lip to keep from smiling. Her voice may sound silly, but he knew what it was like to deal with a broken nose. Not funny.

She cocked her head and gave him a questioning look.

"It's a long story. I'll give you the condensed version on the way back to the station." He took her arm. "Come on."

She shook her head. "Cawed Miss P."

"I'll call her back." He pulled out his phone and punched the number. "Miss P? This is Jake."

"Yes, Detective."

"I've got Mac with me. You don't need to pick her up. Thanks anyway."

"Certainly, Detective." He pressed End and smiled at Mac. Mac sighed.

What was that look for? Women. Would he ever figure them out? He looked over his shoulder at the two officers and Francis. "Ready?"

The detectives and Mac led the way to the cars. Again, Jake and Vic waited until Francis was secured in the squad car before getting into the SUV. Mac sat in the backseat.

Jake swiveled in his seat so he could see Mac's face before relating a short version of what happened with Francis at the interview and the hospital. Silent tears tracked from her amber eyes to her chin as she listened. She made no move to wipe them away.

When they arrived at the police station, he leaped out and ran around to open her door. "I have to make sure Francis Underwood is taken care of, and report to the Chief." He took her arm. "Do you want to stay and wait? Or I can have an officer take you back to Sam's?"

"I could take her back," Vic said.

"I'll stay." She said in a whisper. "Something to eat? Water?"

Jake put his arm around her as they walked in. "Peanut butter crackers okay?"

She nodded.

Vic punched the button for the elevator. "I've got half a ham and cheese sandwich left I didn't eat."

Mac smiled at him.

A split second of jealousy sparked in Jake. Vic got a smile. All he got was a nod. He shook himself. No time for nonsense, but he did love this woman. As they stepped off the elevator, all thoughts of love disappeared. Francis's screams could be heard throughout the precinct.

"I want to see my brother. Where is Thomas?"

"Vic, take Mac to my office and get her something to eat and some water, please." Jake hurried toward the screams.

The Chief stuck his head out of his office door. "What is that infernal racket?"

Jake stopped. "It's Francis Underwood. I promised she could see her brother when we got back from the hospital."

"Then let her see her brother and get her to stop that caterwauling." Chief Baker slammed his door.

Jake jogged to the holding cells, where Francis had a grip on the bars with her face up against them, screaming as loud as she could. He grabbed the bars, shook them, and yelled louder right in her face. "Stop."

Once again, she backed away.

"I'll get him." Jake resumed his normal tone of voice. He went into the hall. "Where is Thomas Underwood?" he asked the officers gathered there.

"Interview Room One."

"Get him and bring him here."

"Yes, sir."

Jake walked back to Francis's cell. "He's coming. He was in an interview room."

She folded her hands in front of her and peered at him.

Time seemed to drag. It wasn't that far from the cells to the interview rooms. Where were they? Finally, he heard footsteps. The haunted face of Thomas Underwood seemed to have aged ten years, and he shuffled through the door like an old man.

"What have you done to him?" Francis leaped to the bars of her cell once more. "Oh, Thomas. Come closer."

He moved slowly across the room. "Francis."

That one word—the saying of her name—seemed to hold so much. Disappointment, frustration, fatigue. And love. How did these two people come from the same parents? In his work,

Jake struggled with that question a lot. Thomas wasn't perfect, but Francis ...

"Thomas, I want you to know that I will support you through all of this. I know you had your reasons for what you did." Francis stretched an arm between the bars toward her brother.

Jake stared at her. "Come on, Francis. It's too late for that. We know you switched the fuses, set the bomb, and killed Laura." He shook his head. "Thomas will be charged with embezzling. That's it."

She fixed Jake with a menacing glare. "My big brother has always taken care of me."

"Not this time, Francis," Thomas said. "I've recanted my confession. It's time you take responsibility for your actions."

"Why you ..." Francis's face flared red. "If daddy were alive, he'd take care of you."

"You were always a daddy's girl, and you learned how to deal with your problems from him. If you can't lie your way out, get rid of them."

"It worked for him." Francis jutted her chin out.

"Until he got caught and sent to prison." Thomas sighed. "Like father, like daughter."

"I guess I'll just have to take care of you when I get out." She narrowed her eyes at her brother. "All of you." She swept her gaze around the room.

Jake's gut knotted up. He'd make sure she never got out.

# CHAPTER 44

Mac crept up behind Vic in the hallway. She peeked around him at the scene playing out in the cells. Francis stood with her face pressed against the bars of her cell, her arm extended as far as she could manage toward her brother, Thomas.

Thomas said something she couldn't catch, but whatever it was, Francis's face hardened into a mask of fury. What had Thomas said?

"Why you ..." Francis's face flared red. "If daddy were alive, he'd take care of you."

Mac shivered as if an icy blast of air rushed at her from the cells. She strained to hear what he said in reply, but he spoke too softly.

Francis's answer was loud and clear. "I guess I'll just have to take care of you when I get out. All of you."

Mac anchored her gaze on Jake's familiar profile. Her hands curled into fists. Not if she had anything to say about it. Nobody messed with her future husband.

"Make arrangements to transport the prisoner to the

county jail." Jake kept his gaze on Francis. "In the meantime, keep Thomas Underwood in an interview room under guard." He turned and headed for the door.

Mac waited against the wall. As he stepped into the hallway, she touched his arm. He turned toward her and she smiled at him, letting her eyes say what she didn't want to speak out loud in a public place.

He sighed and smiled back. "I'm glad you stayed." He waved the papers in his hands. "Vic and I still need to brief the Chief. Then I can leave."

She nodded.

"Why don't you come in with us? He won't mind." He placed a hand on her back and steered her down the hall to the Chief's office.

"Mackenzie." Chief Baker came around his desk and gave her a careful hug. "Get another chair." He waved at Jake and guided Mac to the cushiest chair. "You've been through a lot lately."

"Yesh, shir."

He waved his hand again. "Forget the sir. You don't work for me." He grinned at her. "Although there are many times I wish you did."

She gave him a warm smile that lifted her cheeks. Which moved the tape on her nose and sent pain shooting into her forehead. She winced. No big smiles for a while.

"Did you hear? Ivy's doing so well. She may be released early."

Ivy was Chief Baker's niece and one of Mac's best friends since childhood. She'd been involved with a ruthless man who used her and left her to face the charges, and Mac's friend ended up sentenced to two years at a mental health facility. "I've lost touch with her." Sadness pressed down on Mac like a heavy blanket.

"Don't feel bad." Chief Baker folded his hands on his desk. "She stopped communicating with just about everyone after her dad died. I only heard this because I'm on the list for reports from the doctors."

"Do you think she'll come back to Washington?" Her speech was getting better. Good.

He shrugged. "Her mom's still here."

First Nate came back into her life. Then Zoe. Mac hoped Ivy would. It was good to make new friends, but nice to keep the old ones too. What was that song, about one being silver and the other gold? Turn on the way back machine. Brownies? That was one of the adventures she shared with Ivy.

Jake returned with a chair. "Had to get this one from my office. Where's Vic?"

"Here." Vic plopped into a chair. "The transport arrived for Francis. I made sure she was on it."

"Good. Now we can put Thomas in a cell." Jake rose. "I'll be back."

"Vic, you can get started with the briefing." Chief Baker opened a file on his desk and retrieved a pen from the drawer.

"I'll start with the hospital." Vic consulted his notes.

Vic had gotten to the part where Francis admitted switching the fuses but claimed she hadn't done it to kill Doug when Jake returned.

"She only wanted to hurt him enough so she would have to help him, and he'd notice her." Jake rubbed the back of his neck. "Somehow she thought that would lead to him falling in love with her."

"That's one of the craziest things I've ever heard." The Chief leaned back and linked his hands over his stomach.

"Yeah, but the rest of the story isn't just crazy, it's scary." Jake looked at Vic. "You were doing a good job. Go ahead."

Vic related the rest of what happened at the hospital.

Mac reached for Jake's hand. They'd both come so close to losing their lives at the hand of Francis Underwood.

When Vic finished, the Chief ran a hand over his bald head. "I hope you got this all on tape."

"We did." Vic nodded. "I checked it."

"Good." Chief Baker folded his hands on the desk. "Go home. Tomorrow, I want your written reports on my desk. Along with a transcript of the tape."

Mac gave a sigh of relief. She needed real food, and by that she meant something warm and substantial, and a nap. From the looks of him, Jake could use both those things as well.

"Ready?" He helped her on with her jacket.

She leaned on him all the way to the squad car and didn't complain when he helped her into the back seat. Jake sat up front with the officer driving them back. The ride to Sam's house seemed to take only minutes.

When the car came to a stop, she woke with a start, her head propped against the window. Since she couldn't breathe through her nose, a small puddle of drool wet her jacket in the upper right quadrant. A lump of self-pity formed in her throat.

First, her beautiful hair yanked from her head, then her perfect nose disfigured for life. Jake would probably find someone else and she'd be an old maid.

In the foyer, Jake helped her with her coat. He lifted her face with a finger under her chin. "What's wrong, sweetheart?" He drew her to him with his one good arm.

"I'm ugly." Mac searched Jake's face for the love she so desperately needed to see there.

"Yes, you are." His eyes twinkled with mischief.

She didn't want his jokes. She wanted reassurance. Love. She yanked away from him, but he retained his grip around her.

"But, you're *my* ugly duckling. Who will soon be a beautiful swan again." He nuzzled her neck before kissing her ear. "Does this hurt?"

Ugly duckling, huh? "No." Beautiful swan, she could live with.

"Good." He kissed her jawline. "What about this?"

"No." She pressed against him. This was more like it.

"How about now?" He kissed her with an urgency that left her weak. "I love you." His breath mingled with hers. "I will always love you."

Her heart uncurled its wings and fluttered in her chest. *Thank You, Jesus.*

"Oh good. You two are back." Sam entered from the kitchen. "Are you hungry?"

Jake and Mac looked at Sam, and then at each other.

"Are we hungry?" Jake asked.

"I could eat." In fact, Mac felt great and she was starving.

Jake released her. "Let's eat."

"It's not much. Chili and grilled cheese." Sam turned on her heel.

"Yummy." Mac hurried into the kitchen. "Let me help."

"I'll fix the sandwiches while you dish the chili." Sam handed her the bowls.

The door from the garage opened and Alan came in, rubbing his hands together. "Looks like my timing is perfect." He hung up his coat and crossed to Sam. "Grilled cheese and ...?"

"Chili."

He nuzzled her cheek.

"Go away." Sam waved the spatula at him. "Your nose is cold."

He raised his eyebrows at Jake. "See what happens after a few years of married life?"

"Speaking of which." Sam turned and brandished the spatula at Jake. "Have you two picked a date yet?"

"That depends on my physical therapist." It was Jake's turn to raise his eyebrows at Alan.

"Two weeks and you'll be out of the sling. You should be able to use your arm to some extent. Although we'll have to build the muscle up again."

"I'm the one who'll be holding it up." Mac pointed to her nose. "I may need a bit longer."

Alan held up his hands like he was framing her face for a photo. "A little make-up and you'll be fine."

"Not funny." Mac glared at him.

"Keep in mind when Elizabeth is due, please." Sam patted her stomach.

"Getting back to rehab, it's time you and I disappear into the other room." Alan pointed at Jake.

Jake groaned. "I was hoping for a little nap before."

"You can sleep after." Alan inclined his head toward the exercise room.

"That's all right. Mac and I will take care of the dishes." Sam's sarcasm was lost on her husband. She shook her head. "I believe he does that on purpose to get out of having to clean up."

Mac chuckled. "I can do it. You sit down."

"No. I don't mind when you're helping. It gives us a chance to talk." Sam poured the leftover chili into a bowl. "What happened with Francis today?"

Mac paused her plate stacking. Where should she begin? When she accosted Zoe, Miss P, and her at the office? The office. Mac looked at Sam. "She blew up our office." Tears welled in her eyes.

"I know." Sam slid an arm around her. "It's okay." She laid

her head on Mac's shoulder. "Either we'll rebuild or we'll find another office. We've done it before."

Mac tilted her head so they touched. What would she do without her best friend and partner in her life? "Thank you."

"For what?"

"For always being a ray of sunshine in my life." Mac gazed at their reflections in the window over the sink. One dark head and one blonde. Soul sisters.

The doorbell chimed. Sam looked at the clock and frowned. "I'm not expecting anyone. What about Jake?"

"Not that I know of." Mac trailed Sam down the hall to the front door. "Check through the peephole before opening it."

Sam gave her a "duh" look and pressed her eye against the fishbowl lens. "It's a woman. With a child." She opened the door. "May I help you?"

"I hope so." The skinny woman gathered the young boy to her like a hen protecting her chick. "Are you Samantha Sanders Majors?"

"Yes. Who are you?"

"I'm Elsie." She pushed her long, streaked blonde hair back behind her ears with trembling hands. "My boyfriend, Greg Sanders, said to look you up if I ever had any trouble."

Elsie's gray-green eyes had a haunted look, and the sense of dread surged in Mac again, threatening to drown her. What did this woman want with Sam?

"What's going on?" Jake came up behind them.

The little boy broke free from his mother's grasp. He ran for Jake. "Daddy." He flung himself at Jake, who managed to catch him with his one good arm.

Daddy? Mac stumbled back against the wall and stared at Jake.

Elsie gasped. "You look just like him. Older, but …"

Older than who? What was going on? Mac fought to stay upright.

"This is my brother, Jake." Sam pointed at Jake. "I have no idea who you or this Greg Sanders are. But I don't appreciate you coming here and disrupting my household."

Mac tore her eyes from where the little boy snuggled against Jake's shoulder to look at Elsie.

"You have another brother, my boyfriend, Greg Sanders." Elsie inclined her head toward Jake. "So do you. And I need your help. He's missing."

THE END

# ACKNOWLEDGMENTS

1 Corinthians says, "So whether you eat or drink, or whatever you do, do it all for the glory of God." (ch. 10, vs. 31, NLT) When it comes to writing a book, I've found that requires a lot of help.

First, there are the prayers. I want to thank all my friends and family who faithfully pray me through each book.

On the technical end, I want to thank Detective Lieutenant Steve Sitzes of the Washington Police Department, Washington, Missouri. He takes time out of his day to text with me, talk with me, and we've even met a couple of times. He shares his expertise with me and helps me keep things as true to life as possible. If you find any mistakes in my book, I take complete responsibility!

Thanks to my Word Weaver posse—Bonnie Sue Beardsley, Starr Ayers, Denise Holmberg, Linda Dindzans, Caroline Powers, and Charlsie Estes—for giving me the support and constructive criticism I need to become a better writer and a better person.

Thanks also to DiAnn Mills, Patricia Bradley, and Sandra Melville Hart for always being there when I need you.

And of course, I owe a great deal of gratitude to Linda Fulkerson and the entire Scrivenings Press family. Especially all the wonderful editors. Thank you for all your help.

Most of all, I thank God for my husband, Les. He not only supports my efforts but is my biggest fan. I am blessed.

# ABOUT THE AUTHOR

When Deborah Sprinkle retired from teaching in 2004, she had a plan for keeping busy. Attend the women's Bible study at her church, join a local book club, and write a mystery novel.  She began going to Bible study on Wednesday mornings, and when her local library started a book club, she was one of the charter members.

One thing led to another—as they usually do—and pretty soon she was a Bible study leader and facilitating the book club.

In 2009, she was asked to attend the She Speaks Christian Writers' Conference put on by Proverbs 31 Ministry where she met Kendra Armstrong. It was their friendship that led to her first book, *Exploring the Faith of America's Presidents,* written in collaboration with Kendra.

After attending lots of conferences, taking many classes, and sitting at the feet of a plethora of experienced writers, Deborah wrote her first novel. And, in 2019, her dream came true when *Deadly Guardian* made its debut. Three more novels rounded out the Trouble in Pleasant Valley series, and she now has a new set of mystery novels set in a small town in Missouri called Mac and Sam Mysteries. The first of these is *The Case of the Innocent Husband.*

Originally from St. Louis, Debbie received her bachelor degree in chemistry from the University of Missouri-St. Louis. She worked as a research chemist for many years at both St. Louis University Medical School and Washington University Medical School. In 1991, she and her family moved to Memphis, where Deborah taught chemistry for ten years at a private girls' school before retiring

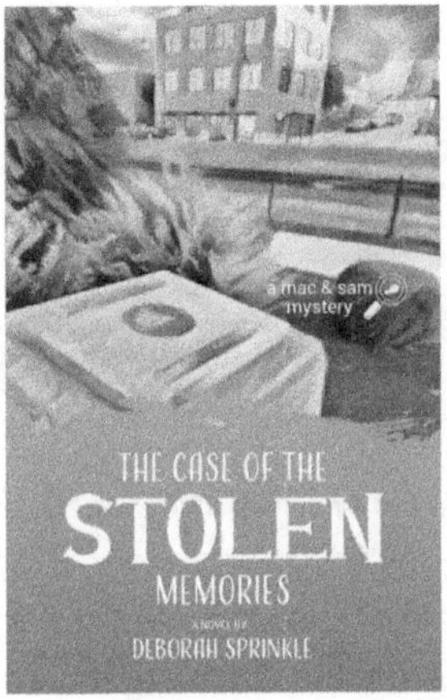


**The Case of the Stolen Memories**

It's the beginning of a new year and Private Investigator Mackenzie Love resolves to get in better shape. But after only one week of walking before work, she interrupts a burglary in progress and ends up in the middle of a murder case.

Detective Jake Sanders, the man Mac's dating, is assigned to the murder, and Mac, along with her partners Samantha Majors and Ms. Prudence Freebody, are hired to find the memorabilia stolen from the time capsule in Rennick Park. The two cases intertwine, and Mac finds herself once more on the wrong end of a gun!

Can Mac and Jake find the killer and the stolen property before the killer finds them?

Get your copy here: https://scrivenings.link/stolenmemories

### *The Case of the Innocent Husband*

Private Investigator Mackenzie Love needs to do one thing. Find out who shot Eleanor Davis. Or she'll have to leave town.

When Eleanor Davis is found shot in her garage, the only suspect, her estranged husband, is found not guilty in a court of law. However, most of the good citizens of Washington, Missouri, remain unconvinced. It doesn't matter that twelve men and women of the jury found him not guilty. What do they know?

And since Private Investigator Mackenzie Love accepted the job for the defense and helped acquit Connor Davis, her friends and neighbors have placed her squarely in the enemy camp. Therefore, her overwhelming goal becomes to find out who killed Eleanor Davis. Or leave the town she grew up in.

As the investigation progresses, the threats escalate. Someone wants to stop Mackenzie and her partner, Samantha Majors, and is willing to do whatever it takes—including murder.

Can Mac and Sam find the killer before they each end up on the wrong side of a bullet?

Get your copy here: https://scrivenings.link/innocenthusband

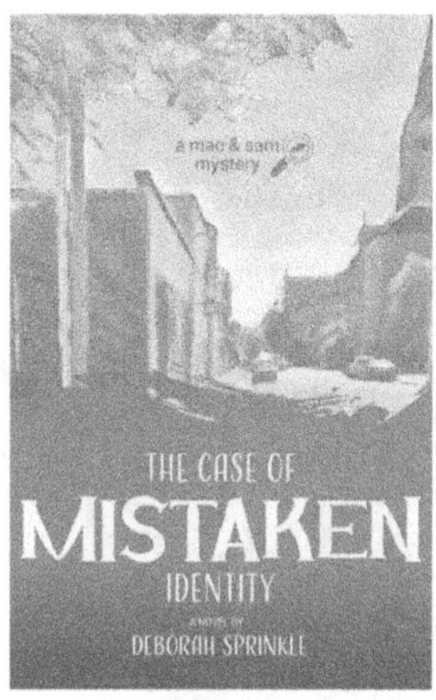


### *The Case of Mistaken Identity*

Private Investigator Mackenzie Love manages to get into trouble on a simple shopping trip where she finds herself at the business end of a gun. It's clear her attacker mistakes her for someone else, but who? And why is her look-alike in so much trouble?

Mac enlists the help of her partners, Samantha Majors and Miss P, and Detective Jake Sanders to find her doppelgänger and solve the case of mistaken identity.

In the meantime, Mr. Fischer of Fischer Industries comes to the private detectives for help with a problem of his own. As Mac and Sam work on his case, they begin to wonder if the two cases are related.

Can Mac and Sam unravel the clues and get justice for both Mac's look-alike and Mr. Fischer?

Get your copy here: https://scrivenings.link/mistakenidentity

### *The Case of the Stolen Memories*

It's the beginning of a new year and Private Investigator Mackenzie Love resolves to get in better shape. But after only one week of walking before work, she interrupts a burglary in progress and ends up in the middle of a murder case.

Detective Jake Sanders, the man Mac's dating, is assigned to the murder, and Mac, along with her partners Samantha Majors and Ms. Prudence Freebody, are hired to find the memorabilia stolen from the time capsule in Rennick Park. The two cases intertwine, and Mac finds herself once more on the wrong end of a gun!

Can Mac and Jake find the killer and the stolen property before the killer finds them?

Get your copy here: https://scrivenings.link/stolenmemories

# TROUBLE IN PLEASANT VALLEY

**Deadly Guardian**

**Trouble in Pleasant Valley**—*Book One*

Madison Long, a high school chemistry teacher, looks forward to a relaxing summer break. Instead, she suffers through a nightmare of threats, terror, and death. When she finds a man murdered she once dated, Detective Nate Zuberi is assigned to the case, and in the midst of chaos, attraction blossoms into love.

Together, she and Nate search for her deadly guardian before he decides the only way to truly save her from what he considers a hurtful relationship is to kill her—and her policeman boyfriend as well.

Get your copy here:

https://scrivenings.link/deadlyguardian

**Death of an Imposter**

**Trouble in Pleasant Valley**—*Book Two*

Her first week on the job and rookie detective Bernadette Santos has been given the murder of a prominent citizen to solve. But when her victim turns out to be an imposter, her straight forward case takes a nasty turn. One that involves the attractive Dr. Daniel O'Leary, a visitor to Pleasant Valley and a man harboring secrets.

When Dr. O'Leary becomes a target of violence himself, Detective Santos has two mysteries to unravel. Are they related? And how far can she trust the good doctor? Her heart tugs her one way while her mind pulls her another. She must discover the solutions before it's too late!

Get your copy here:

https://scrivenings.link/deathofanimposter

**Silence Can Be Deadly**

**Trouble in Pleasant Valley—***Book Three*

Forced from the career he loved and into driving a taxi, Peter Grace had grown accustomed to his simple life. Until one night when a suspicious fare and a traffic jam blew it all apart, and he was on the run again. Only this time it wasn't a matter of changing occupations but of life and death.

He needed help and he knew where to find it. His old friend Rafe in Pleasant Valley. What he didn't count on was finding not only the help he needed but a community of new friends and the love of his life. Zoe Poole.

The story of Captain Nate Zuberi and his wife Madison continues as they, too, risk their lives to help Peter. Along with Peter, Rafe, and Zoe, they strive to catch an assassin.

But can the group of friends find the killer before anyone else gets hurt?

Get your copy here:

https://scrivenings.link/silencecanbedeadly

<br>


*Death Under the Ice*

**Trouble in Pleasant Valley**—*Book Four*

When Homeland Security Analyst Claire Green's brother urges her to visit, she clears her desk in Chicago and heads for southern Ohio. But when she arrives, the house is deserted and her brother is missing.

Claire enlists the help of her brother's neighbors in the quest to find him, but she's in for two surprises.

First, Alan has been keeping secrets from her—secrets that may have gotten him killed, and put her life in danger.

Second, Private Investigator Rafe O'Connell, the only man she ever loved—and lost—is a close friend of Madison and Nate's, and they ask him to be part of the investigation.

Claire needs their help, but can she put past hurts behind her as she not only tries to find her brother, but stay alive?

Get your copy here:

https://scrivenings.link/deathundertheice

# ALSO BY DEBORAH SPRINKLE

**Trinity Sands Beach Club**

*A collection of Romantic Suspense novellas*

**What do a widow, a newly divorced woman, and a retired professor
of art history have in common?**

They all came to Trinity Sands Island to find a simple life without any
entanglements. But instead, they are each confronted with a mystery
and another chance at romance. Will they be brave enough to face the
possible dangers of solving a mystery and of losing their hearts?

**This collection includes three novellas:**

**"Trinity Sands Treasure Hunt" by Sharon Carpenter**

Retired art professor Claire Anderson inherited all of her uncle's
worldly goods.  Arriving at his Trinity Sands Beach Club bungalow,
she faces the daunting task of sorting through the boxes and bags that
he left behind.

When someone tries to break in and steal seemingly worthless items, Claire calls Chief of Security, Ben Hastings and sparks fly. Claire and Ben realize all is not as it seems when they set out to discover who is targeting the house.

In their search for answers, will the attraction between Claire and Ben deepen into real treasure?

**_"SeaBreeze Obsession"_ by Jen Dodrill**

Newly single Karah Halyard returns to her beach cottage and starts "SeaBreeze Designs," a business specializing in beach decor. But beneath the tentative peace of her life, unresolved feelings stir as she considers reconciling with her ex-husband, Gage, who is in town doing research.

When a secret admirer confronts her on the beach, Karah defends herself and runs. That night, he's found dead. As she and Gage face a murder investigation, they must confront their past and unravel the mystery of the real killer.

Can they solve the crime and reconcile their fractured relationship?

**_"Searching for Serenity"_ by Deborah Sprinkle**

Grace Caldwell hasn't been to their beach house since her husband passed away three years ago. Her grief has kept her from moving forward with her life. But when a letter arrives from her friend, Serenity James, saying something strange is going on at the Beach Club, Grace decides it's time to head south. However, when she arrives, Serenity has disappeared, and no one knows where she is.

Detective Peter Young gets involved and, as Grace and he work together, a mutual attraction blossoms—one that takes Grace by surprise.

Will Grace find love again while solving the mystery behind Serenity's disappearance?

**Sharktooth Island**

*A collection of Romantic Suspense novellas*

**A fabled island that no one dares to tame.**

**This collection contains four novellas:**

***Book 1 - Out of the Storm*** *(1830)* by Susan Page Davis

Laura Bryant sails with her father and his three-man crew on his small coastal trading schooner. After a short stay in Jamaica, where she meets Alex Dryden, an officer on another ship, the Bryants set out for their home in New England.

In a storm, they are blown off course east of Savannah, Georgia, to a foreboding island. Captain Bryant tells his daughter he's heard tales of that isle. It's impossible to land on, though it looks green and inviting from a distance. It has no harbor but is surrounded by dangerous rocks and cliffs.

Pirates outrun the storm and decide to bury a cache of treasure on this island and return for it later. On board is Alex, whom the cutthroats captured in Jamaica and forced to work for them. Alex risks his own life to escape the pirates and tries to help Laura and Captain Bryant outwit them. Beneath the deadly struggle, romance blossoms for Laura.

### Book 2 - *A Passage of Chance* (1893) by Linda Fulkerson

Orphaned at a young age, Melody Lampert longs to escape the loveless home of the grandmother who begrudgingly raised her. Stripped of her inheritance due to her grandmother's resentments, Melody discovers her name remains on the deed of one property—an obscure island off the Georgia coast that she shares with her cousin. But when he learns the island may contain a hidden pirate treasure, he's determined to cheat her out of her share.

Ship's mechanic Padric Murphy made a vow to his dying father—break the curse that has plagued their family for generations. To do so, he must return what was taken from Sharktooth Island decades earlier—a pair of rare gold pieces. His opportunity to right the wrong arrives when his new employer sets sail to explore the island.

After a series of unexplainable mishaps occur, endangering Padric and his boss's beautiful cousin Melody, he fears his chance of breaking the curse may be ruined. But is the island's greed thwarting his plans? Or the greed of someone else?

### Book 3 - *Island Mayhem* (1937) by Elena Hill

Louise Krause stopped piloting to pursue nursing, but when money got too tight she was forced to give up her dreams and start ferrying around a playboy who managed to excel during the Great Depression. When a routine aerial tour turns south, Louise is unable to save the plane.

After crash landing, the cocky pilot is stranded. She longs to escape the uninhabited island, but her makeshift raft sinks, and she and her companions are in even worse trouble. Can Louise learn to trust the others in order to survive, or will the island's curse and potential sabotage lead to her demise?

**Book 4 - *After the Storm*** *(present day)* by Deborah Sprinkle

Mercedes Baxter inherited two passions from her father—a love for Sharktooth Island, a spit of land in the middle of the ocean left to her in his will, and a dedication to the study of the flora and fauna on and around its rocky landscape.

For the last five years, since graduating from college, Mercy led a peaceful, simple life on the island with only her cat, Hawkeye, for company. Through grant money she obtained from a conservancy in Savannah, she could live on her island while studying and writing about the plants and animals there. Life was perfect.

But when a hurricane hits the island, Mercy's life changes for good. Her high school sweetheart, Liam Stewart, shows up to help her with repairs, and ignites the flame that has never quite died away. And if that's not enough, while assessing the damage to the island, they make a discovery that puts both their lives in danger.

*Stay up-to-date on your favorite books and authors with our free e-newsletters.*

ScriveningsPress.com